TOMAHAWKS & SORCERY

Airship 27 Productions

Published by Airship 27 Productions
www.airship27.com
www.airship27hangar.com

Managing Editor: Ron Fortier
Associate Editor: Gordon Dymowski
Marketing and Promotions Manager: Michael Vance
Production Designer: Rob Davis

ISBN: 978-1-969285-09-7

Produced in the United States of America

10 9 8 7 6 5 4 3 2 1

TOMAHAWKS
& SORCERY

Teel James Glenn

TABLE OF CONTENTS

Dedication:

To Fess Parker—who gave me a love for buckskin adventures and Robert Ervin Howard who took me to far worlds and let me join in the fun

Acknowledgement:

Again, to The Group—Nancy, Lee, Wayne and Jaime—my writing family. And ET—who always supports.

DEVIL OF THE DEEP WOODS

PROLOGUE

WARNING FROM THE PAST

Declinn was deep in the nightmare again. It was the same as it always, exactly, but then that was to be expected because it was as much a memory of things that had happened as the gut-wrenching emotions, he had experienced during them.

The memory always began at the same point:

Declinn Blayde ran until he thought his lungs would burst from the strain and then pushed himself to run some more.

He was a tall man dressed in a ragged uniform, now torn and muddied by his flight. He had a broad chest, wide shoulders and narrow waist. His long black hair was held back with a rawhide band and flowed behind him as he ran. His ruggedly handsome face was now contorted with fear, his grey eyes swirling pools of conflict.

The full moon had crawled behind a cloud leaving him to grope his way through the forest trail at reckless speed as he tried to get away from the pursuing Huron.

Declinn swatted branches out of his way and was finally forced to slow to a fast walk. He dared not rest so he pushed forward, brushing into the rough surface of many trees.

He no longer gave thought to the why or the how of the thing that had happened to him as he raced through the darkness through the pine forest. *Has it only been two days ago that I discovered what the damned French were going to do?*

It was a Mohican holy man who, in the midst of a trance had told Declinn that a dark horror was to come, and the frontier scout had been living with the native tribes too long to dismiss any of their magick or such pronouncements.

I have to get to them and warn them!

He realized he couldn't distract himself with abstract thoughts, he had to confine himself to survival on a minute-to-minute basis.

Declinnn made it to the edge of the tree line to a clearing just as the gibbous moon cleared a cloud and sent its orange light across the scene. Ahead of him down a long slope of the hill were Fort William Henry and the glassy surface of Lake George beyond. It was a hot August night in 1757 and the Fort had been under siege for days.

The French emplacements around the fort and the boom of cannons told the entire story. It was more than Blayde wanted to know; his arrival was almost too late.

The walls of the fort, though never intended to withstand canon fire, were thick with log facings around an earthen filling to give them substance. The bombards would batter those walls down unless General Webb, the commander at Fort Edward sent a relief column. And Blayde knew that was not going to happen.

The fort was intended to house four to five hundred men, but those numbers were swollen when the siege began, with additional troops that had quartered in an entrenched camp southeast of the fort flooding in.

Blayde searched for an alternative way to the fort, for moving out on to the slope would expose his shape in the bright moonlight. Any keen eyes that happened to scan up toward the hill would have no difficulty targeting him. Even his green wool jacket— uniform of the Roger Rangers— would not be enough to hide him from the eyes of the Huron or Algonquin allies of the French.

Still, the lone man knew he had to try to make the run for the fort or those hunting him in the woods would find him. He really was between the proverbial rock and a hard place.

The fort was surrounded on three sides by a dry moat, with the fourth side sloping down to the lake. The only access to the fort was by a bridge across the moat.

If Blayde could get to the moat, he knew they would let him in when he gave the call sign. He knew he was fighting destiny, for the holy man had said the blood and death was *going* to happen, and the woodsman believed in that native magicks. Still, Declinn had to try to at least add his gun to the defenders.

Inside the fort were wooden barracks two stories high, built around the parade ground. Blayde knew that because of the heavy bombardment and siege operations that progressively neared the fort's walls, the garrison would eventually be forced to surrender when they got the news that Webb would not send any relief.

He also knew there were women and children huddled in that fort.

More pointedly he knew that the British and their camp followers would be told they would be allowed to withdraw, under French escort to Fort Edward on condition that they refrain from participation in the war for 18 months. They would be allowed to keep their muskets but no ammunition, and a single symbolic canon. Declinn knew it would not be enough to save them.

I have to warn them that the General Montcalm's force have no intention to stop their Indian allies, Declinn thought, *I have to stop it, it will be a massacre.* He had heard the talk among the French officers while concealed beneath a woodpile. They fully intended to allow their allies full reign because they feared if they did not the red men would turn on them afterward. It would be just as the holy man had predicted.

The British force would be slaughtered when they came out of the fort. They would not be able to stop the mad rush of the French's Indian allies who did not practice the limited and artificially honorable war of the Europeans. The Indians knew only the concept of total destruction of the enemy in combat and so would sweep in and put the marching English to the knife.

Blayde had been running through the woods for two days to try and stop it.

I know its insane, he thought, *Munro will never believe me—he is too 'civilized' a soldier to think men in uniforms would allow such a thing, happen but he doesn't know how savage the French are, just not the honest savagery of the Indians. I have to stop it now. I have to make him hold out despite Webb's refusal to help.*

The frontiersman had no idea how he would make it though the French force's camps to the south and west of the fort to persuade the British commander, but he had to try.

He waited for another cloud to skitter across the moon and then made a break down the slope. He thought he'd made it clear to the brush below but just as he reached the bottom of the incline, he heard the sound of movement behind him.

The Huron that had been chasing him all night had found his scent!

Blayde continued his headlong flight, ducking and dodging branches as his powerful long legs launched him through the thick underbrush. He abandoned caution now, mindless of the French ahead of him for the 'hounds' on his tail were devoted to his death. Branches snapped before him or whipped him across the face and upthrust arms as his run became more desperate.

Declinn pulled away from the Hurons on the flat plane of the valley floor. He found a hunting trail and moved onto it to make better time. Soon, however, he heard the Indians gaining.

There were only two of them from the sound of their footfalls and Blayde decided that if he was to confront them now, he might still make it. *I only have to make it through the eight thousand French troops ahead of me*, Declin thought wryly.

The green clad ranger drew the tomahawk from his belt and positioned himself behind a wide tree trunk at the side of the trail and waited. He fought to catch his breath and calm himself, to clear his mind to be ready to fight.

It's just me and them, he thought. *All wars come down to this: just men face to face.* Then he put all thoughts of philosophy out of his mind to concentrate on survival.

Abruptly the first of the trackers, a long limbed Huron raced past the tree, eyes on the ground to look for sign in the now brighter moonlight.

Blayde let him pass and waited, holding his breath until the second brave darted by.

Then the 'hare' swung at the 'hound' and in two vicious strikes from his tomahawk the second pursuer was dead.

The first brave turned on the sound of the attack but before he could even start back Blayde had thrown his weapon and the steel blade of the tomahawk bit deeply into the chest of the Huron.

Blayde snatched up his first victim's hatchet and was about to resume his run when a third Indian— one he had not heard— slammed into his back.

The two of them went rolling in the dirt as the ranger tried to get his weapon to bear but failed.

The Huron straddled Declinn and before he could react the Indian thrust the long blade of a hunting knife at the ranger's chest.

Blayde managed to twist to take the deep thrust to the meat of his left shoulder. The frontiersman grunted with the pain but now that the knife was in him he twisted back so violently that he tore the weapon from the Huron's grasp.

The move so startled the Indian brave that Declinn was able to heave the red man off him and then roll atop him. Then Blayde pulled the knife from his shoulder and plunged it into the beating heart of the Huron.

As the light of life faded from the Indian's eyes Blayde was puzzled that saw nothing but triumph in the warrior's expression. Blayde suddenly knew he was right, because the shock of the brave's knife attack on him caught up with the frontiersman then.

Blayde felt his limbs go numb and his vision began to swim. The bombards exploding over the fort echoed in his head and he knew with a sickening feeling in his stomach that the Huron trackers had won. He knew he wouldn't make it to the fort, wouldn't stop the assault or the inevitable surrender.

Blayde fell forward over the man he had killed and passed out until long after the slaughter at Fort William Henry went forward just as predicted…

Now Blayde woke in cold sweat from the memory-nightmare, as he always did. He shivered, despite the warm air as he remembered the bloody carnage of the aftermath of the fort siege.

Every day since then he had felt like he could have done more: if only had had run faster, if only he had been stronger, if only he had heard the third brave. If he could have shaken off that knife wound. If only.

He found solace in his sculpting work, but the guilt, like the scar on his shoulder, was always with him. Little did he know that the nightmare would come back to haunt him in the daylight…

CHAPTER ONE

THE FIRE IN THE DEEP

The Huron homelands were known as Ouendake, which loosely translates to 'home of the island dwellers.' Ouendake was surrounded by water, making river and lake travel an essential part of everyday life in Huronia. Canoes flowed freely along the waterways and paths along the banks showed frequent passage between the scattered villages to keep the peoples connected to one another.

The Huron nation lived in the shadow of the Other Folk, those who lived in the caves of the underworld and the Sky Ones who walked the clouds above all. Thus, The People were always in a middle place between the warring forces of the gods of darkness and light. Yet the Huron all practiced the sacred rituals that made sure that helped them to live in balance with the world.

Then the White Skins came from the land across the great waters and brought with them a different way of living and thinking, both ways that made little sense. The French, unlike the English were relatively wise in their dealings with The People, in that the let them live their lives much as they had before.

But the British, sworn enemies of the French, decried the Gods of the Huron, belittled their customs and took the land that was the free right of all. These arrogant British claimed the land for their own, as if any of the middle realm could actually own the land that was the gift to all.

For years the British called English and the French contented for supremacy in and around the land of Ouendake, sometimes violently, sometimes peacefully warring with words and treaties (which they freely broke), while the world continued to spin. Neither side seemed to ever gain any advantage in the continual struggle.

Then the French and English settled their fight in far away land called Europe and those who had allied themselves with the French were suddenly told they should have to serve the English. They were ordered to follow the English way of doing things. The arrogant British leader called Sir Jeffery Amherst made it known that old treaties and annual gifts to honor chiefs and gods were to be discontinued.

The Prophet of The Delaware preached a return to the old way and the great Pontiac raised an army to fight against the whites. Many knives were bloodied, and the war hatchet drank deeply in many skulls. But some who fought the invaders did so with even darker weapons then the bloody tomahawk.

From the darkest of the deep woods the echoes reached the settlements of the British of a new native prophet, one who was leading the Huron (who the English often called the Wyandot). He was commanding them down dangerous and horrible paths that led straight to Hell. With the echoes of that name came the screams of the damned and the cackle of unholy laughter that lingered even in the bright sunlight of midday.

+++

Willow Creek Settlement was a group of twenty families that had pushed further into the wilderness than other settlers even as the war with the French was being fought not so far away. There they found a lush valley with a gentle stream flowing through it, and good, fertile bottom land bordered by forests full of rich timbers. They had established a common storeroom/blockhouse on the shore of Willow Creek first then spread out across the valley to individual homesteads. They had cleared land and planted the first crops only two years before, while the war with the French still raged. Now, in 1765, with peace declared, there was hope for prosperity in this newly won valley.

It was a hard life, carving an existence from the wilderness, but they were all committed to the thought of having something of their own, some part of this new land that would belong to them and that they would belong to. To establish roots and leave a legacy for the generations to come.

It looked to be a good season, with the ground not too hard from the late frost and plenty of water from the mountain runoff keeping the creek level high and the crops watered.

It looked to be a good life.

Deirdre Collins came to Willow Creek with the second wave of settlers, following her husband, a lay minister, who had come with the first. The minister had built a small cabin for the two of them and when time permitted, they hoped to build an actual church as well—until then they held services in the communal storage house which was the ad hoc center of the settlement.

That is where she was with most of the community when the first hint that there was something wrong happened. It was the silence.

Just after the group had finished singing a hymn and Deirdre's husband, Deacon Jacob Collins was rising to begin a sermon she noticed the strangeness in that in that moment of silence. There were only the sounds of the shifting bodies on the wooden benches in the now empty storehouse, but no other sounds.

No bird sang outside, no insects chirped. There even no sound of the breeze moving the tree branches. It was a silence so complete as to be unnatural.

Deirdre thought it odd. She would not have noticed, save that it was so suddenly silent, so completely void of life.

The others noticed a moment after Deirdre and all began to look around, their frontier senses sharpened to impending danger. These were people who were in tune with the land, with its ebbs and flows, with the rhythm of the life that lived there. And now that rhythm was broken.

A moment later the men moved to reach for their rifles, stacked near the door, but by then it was already too late!

Dozens of Huron warriors exploded into the building, tomahawks raised in bloody promise.

The settlement men met the attack with whatever was at hand, several with knives or tomahawks that they had sheathed on their belts. The swarming natives did not brandish rifles themselves, however, using only war-clubs and tomahawks.

The combat was bloody but strange, for while the Huron fought with their usual all-in savagery and the settlers with the desperation men and women fighting for their very existence, the Huron seemed to not be trying to kill. In several instances, when they struck down a settler, they did not follow up with a deathblow. They seemed content to disable.

The natives worked at overwhelming the settlers, striking the men with clubs or strangling them into submission, but did not use their knives or tomahawks for the final killing blows. It was inevitable that with the brutality of the encounters some of the settlers died but the Huron seemed to make a deliberate effort not to kill.

The women and children, despite their screaming terror were not passive observers. They attacked the Huron as well, but the braves almost casually threw them off with brutal distain, though did not follow through with killing blows.

In a far too few minutes the entire surviving population of the settlement was unconscious or subdued. Ten were dead, as were four of the attacking Hurons.

And when the violence was done, in the new unnatural stillness, the skeletal figure of an old Huron walked into the common house. He wore a ceremonial feathered cloak and had a long scalplock on his baldhead decorated with eagle feathers. This wizened figure stood in the doorway, surveying the carnage then broke out into a long, odd laugh that sounded not unlike a predator's cackle.

"Nadia is pleased," the old man said in his language. "And I, Karkuk his instrument am as well. Tonight begins the end of the invasion of white race on our sacred lands!" He turned to the native warriors who stood in worshipful silence, and said, "Bring this refuse outside so ceremony of blood may begin!"

CHAPTER TWO

THE IMAGE OF A GODDESS.

"Touch those again wench," the deep male voice said, "and by God's garters you'll regret it."

The nearly naked, voluptuous young girl he had spoken to laughed, "How will I regret it, my lord?"

"I'll smack your hand and spank your little butt, you forest imp; those are my tools— you should never touch a man's tools." The speaker was Declinn Blayde, with his long, jet-black hair hanging loosely over his broad, muscular shoulders. He was stripped to the waist and despite the cool breeze that blew up the valley onto the slight hill where he chose to work, he was covered in sweat. Save for tanned face and hands his skin was pale. A network of scars crossed his back and arms, arrow and bullet wounds testament to surviving a hard life.

He held a large wooden mallet and a soft nosed steel chisel in strong, expressive hands that seemed almost at odds with his muscular physique for their delicacy. The work he was doing was carving an image on a large panel of wood. It was a bas-relief image of a forest scene and depicted the classical figure of Diana, Goddess of the Hunt. The Goddess' form was very much a mirror of the teen girl before him.

"But I want to touch your tool, Declinn, really I do." The girl's voice was working to be coy. She had auburn hair and the curves with the promise of womanhood that were as new and exciting to her as they were to most of the boys in the village before whom she paraded them every chance she got.

She was dressed in little more than a yard length of cloth wound round her to simulate the diaphanous clothes of the goddess she was modeling for.

"You need to leave *all* my tools alone, Millie," The sculptor said in an amused tone, "I promised I'd bring you back to your father the same way I brought you out here." He alternately looked up at the barely clad girl then switched his focus on the perfected image of her he had sculpted in the rare wood of the alter plate that he was carving.

The alter plate was the size of a table and depicted the goddess offering protection to the beasts of the field and her human followers as quoted from classical references. It was the last of a triptych that Declinn had created over the last months. The wooden plaque would rest behind an altar in a far off Boston College.

"I won't tell daddy if you won't." She leaned up from her reclining position on the couch he had brought to the clearing for her to use. Her act made sure the cloth slipped down just enough to reveal her apple-sized breasts.

"Don't move," he said sharply, "I've almost finished the line of your neck; it's the little details that matter, girl. That's where the devil lives, in the details." He applied himself to recreating the delicate curve with his concentration absolute. His long-fingered hands, that looked as if they should be crushing rocks, now assumed the aspect of a surgeon's as he adjusted the image of the reclining goddess.

The hand of the Goddess' image was extended toward some birds holding the rose that was her symbol. The birds were so perfectly rendered that a viewer would expect to see the flutter of the wings.

The girl, properly chastised by the artist, returned to her frozen position with her hand extended. She had been modeling for him for weeks, each day journeying out to the hilltop he had chosen for the light and the quiet to sit for a couple of hours. At first, he just sketched the girl, then scraped the wooden slab to prepare it for his sculpting. Her father had given permission when the sculptor asked as much for the reason of the commission as for the money she was being paid.

"Declinn is the greatest artist in the colonies, girl" her father had said, "His work is even known in the old-world capitals!"

"But you said he's just an old wood hermit?" She protested. Secretly she was delighted the famous woodsman chose her to model. It would make all the settlement girls jealous; they all thought the tall dark, brooding figure of the artist was attractive, in a dangerous way. She knew though, that if she did not protest her father would think her a hussy, so she made objections he was forced to counter.

"Never mind what I said," her father reprimanded, "He is— but he has honors as well from the first frontier war. You just do what he says within the bounds of propriety: he's paying enough to get us that new plow this year— and you a new dress.'

She didn't care about the plow, but she had plans for the new dress!

"Stop squirming, girl," Declinn said, bringing her back from her daydream, "I'm almost done."

She assumed her position again and tried to stay frozen.

"Declinn, can I ask you a question?"

"Do I have a choice?"

"Why did you come here?"

"The light is good all day here," he said without hesitation, "and the bugs mostly stay off this hill."

"No," she said, "I mean to Kingsborough settlement? We are such a little nowhere of a place. I heard papa call it a backwater." Her serious tone made him look up with human eyes, not an artist's vision to look at the puzzlement on her sweet face.

"You dislike it so much out here? Isn't it a beautiful and serene place?"

"Not really dislike it. Its just that it is all I've ever known except for a trip to Albany when I was eight. I mean, you could have gone anywhere—papa says you could make a living in even the big cities on the coast where it's civilized."

"I like the quiet," he said seriously, "except when models prattle on." She made a pouting face at him. "And I have little use for 'civilized living.' But even a lone wolf will visit the pack once in a while to remind him he is one of them."

"Is it true you lived with the Indians?"

He set one steel chisel aside and took up a smaller one to make a small adjustment on the shoulder of the Goddess' image. He ran a finger of the sculpted curve and took a deep breath as if touching the wood directly was a sensual thing. "I grew up on the north frontier; my father was a trapper. We wintered with the Mohican tribe for a few years; it was their holy mask maker that first taught me to hold a chisel, to learn to love the touch and feel of wood. To see the images inside and bring them out. They consider art to be a gift from the Sky People."

"And they didn't take your scalp?"

"They only do that to the dead now so they can find their way into the hunting ground of the afterlife. And it was the French that taught that to them, anyhow. Now be quiet; I want to finish this so those dressed up fools in the Church can mumble in front of it and feel important." He turned his attention once more to a fine detail.

"If you don't think much of church ceremony, why are you making an alter panel as a gift?"

"Just 'cause I don't think much of the trappings doesn't mean I don't hold with the ideas," he said quietly while he worked. "Seems to me that if you spend enough time in the deep woods you come to know there are forces beyond man out there in the dark. Don't hurt one to look for ways to talk with them forces, lots of different ways to talk to them, lots of different languages just as valid." He shrugged and added, "I just don't see how a lot of pomp makes much sense to whatever those forces are."

"You don't think most city folk ways make much sense, do you?"

"Nope."

"Even settlement folk?"

"They ought to know better," he said leaving in to blow some shavings off the cheek of the Goddess' image, then taking a polishing clothe to the work. "Living close to the deep woods and all, they should hear those voices from the forest loud and clear, but they don't. Pretension to be city folk I guess."

"Papa said once you were more deep-woods savage than settler— says you're almost an Indian yourself."

Declinn grunted with a sound that had humor in it. "Your da's a wise man. Stop moving your head, minx, I'm almost done."

He gave a last gentle tap to the steel chisel then stepped away from the panel looking at it and then the girl with a squinting eye.

"Done!" he said with a deep sigh that hinted at exhaustion. "You can put your clothes on now." He moved to the stump he had been using as a table and slipped the chisel into a strap in his open side pack beside his other chisels were kept and lashed it in.

The girl leapt off her couch and ran around to stare at the panel mindless of how much skin she exposed before she got her drapery under control.

"Oh, Declinn, it's wonderful!" She said with genuine delight. She studied the supine form on the panel; the animals gathered around it the images of men, women and children suggested by the subtle chisel strokes behind the raised figure of the goddess.

"Do I really look like that?" she asked with both wonder and pride in her tone. He had not let her see the work all the weeks he labored on it, fearful he said, that "*You could put on airs or, worse, believe my work.*"

"That is you as you are now, young one, only now made immortal." He took an oiled cloth and began to rub the freshly worked surface of the artwork all over. "When you're old and fat and surrounded with a gaggle of children you'll be able to point to it and show the innocence you were and you'll inspire prayers and smiles for a long time to come with this, I reckon."

"I won't get fat," she pouted. The girl let her cloth drop to the ground around her feet and boldly stepped forward to display a body that seemed to make a lie off any future plumpness.

"Girl—" he said with an exasperated noise. "You are playing with some fire right now that you have no knowledge of and you're gonna get burned one of these days."

She stepped up to him and pressed her naked breasts against the sculptor's equally bare stomach. She looked up into his eyes and suddenly her breath was coming in gasps as if she had been running hard. "Then teach me how put out a fire."

He stared at her with a ferocity that both scared and excited her. For a long moment she held her breath as she stared up at him with earnest eyes. Then he laughed softly.

This made her angry and she slapped him on the chest and backed away with an angry growl. "You are a very mean man!"

"And you are very determined and capable young miss. I'm sure this little set back won't stop you learning all you want—and much more—from the settlement lads. And woe to them for the cost of the lessons they'll get from you!" He reached over and captured her chin between his fingers and thumb and tilted her head up to smile down at her. "You are a right little vixen, Millie my dear and a good one—don't be put off by my refusal; you need both more and less than I can give to you. It wouldn't be fair to either of us to start a fire this way."

Before she could ask him what he meant they became aware of a figure running up the path from the direction of the settlement. When the figure caught sight of them, he began to yell.

"Master Declinn," the running boy screamed. "They say Willow Creek has been wiped out. The Wyandot are on the move; the Fort Commander says to come real fast!"

By the time the boy had made it up to a distance where he didn't have to shout to be heard the sculptor had scooped up his tools in his pack and thrown a canvas tarp over the plaque he'd been working on. The boy stood stunned as Millie donned her clothes with just enough tardiness to give him a hint of what he might have seen if he had been a faster runner.

"Put your eyes in your head, boy,' the artist said, "and bring the wood panel into town with you. If you drop it, I'll skin you alive." He turned to smile at the still pouting model.

"And you supervise him, Millie; after all it's your immortality he's holding in his hands."

This made the girl giggle, and she blew Declinn a kiss to say all was forgiven. By the time the boy had gathered his wits and his burden the sculptor was already halfway down the hill, his long legs pounding at a distance eating run. He headed for the stockade with an urgency and a muttered, "Not again," and remembered visions of horror preceding him.

CHAPTER THREE

THE DARK GOD DESCENDS

The smoke from the burning buildings spread above the Willow Creek Valley in a dense fog that stung the eyes and muffled the cries of the tortured souls trapped beneath it. The light in the eastern sky was pale pink with false dawn and with the flames of the burning huts of English settlements reflected off the layer of smoke it cast a hellish red glow overall. It illuminated, in stark relief, a scene that might have been from the darkest corner of Hell.

"Do what you want with us, monster, you will not break our spirit," the pain wracked survivor of the settlement cried in a hoarse voice. He was bound to a wooden stake driven into the red clay of the earth in front of his burnt and destroyed farmhouse, "You'll get no satisfaction from this horrid abomination before the eyes of God!"

An answer to the prisoner's challenge came only as a twisted laugh from out of the smoke. It seemed a song played on pipes never meant for such a tune and wrapped itself around the prisoner like a spirit snake.

There were twenty-nine other pitiful victims tied, like the first, to stakes driven into the ground in a long line. They were clearly farmers, rough-hewn men of the earth who had been abused badly, tortured as only the Huron could, many bleeding from wounds. The line of staked men stretched down the center of the road that ran through the dying settlement of Willow Creek.

Nearby the bound men were a group of children and women held on their knees by a clot of savage painted warriors. They were the rest of the survivors of the destroyed settlement that had endured a night of uncertainty as the savage Huron had celebrated the total destruction of the village. Each of the women and children had been terrorized by the all-night torture of their men they had witnessed, and each was yoked with rope to each other to prevent them from fleeing.

There was a small army of savage figures that might have come directly from the gates of the damned place itself lording over the kneeling women. These were warrior figures dressed only in breech clothes, with eagle feathers braided in their long black hair and their clan tattoos and war paint clearly visible against their bronzed skin.

There were Huron warriors from many clans united behind the cackling wizened figure that stood at their head. He was more fantastic than any of his followers, skeletal thin with leathered skin and wild, multi-colored tattoos whose headdress was of rare feathers and shells in intricate patterns. He raised his thin arms as he spoke to the staked-out prisoners.

"You will die to the glory of the Huron," the old man who led the warriors said, "and in doing so will bring to this frail form of Karkuk the means to drive all other white skins from our land forever, French and British alike." The old shaman stepped forward and took a long, curved knife to the neck of the first farmer in single, long slice. One of the painted warriors raced up with an ornately carved wooden bowl and placed it beneath the wound to let the gushing blood flow pour into it.

A wailing went up from the group of women and children. They continued to cry in horror as one by one their men were slaughtered before them with prayer and ceremony. The ritual murder was repeated with all the men in the line until almost thirty vessels were full of the sanguine liquid and the surviving villagers had no tears left. All they had were the indelible images of abomination that would haunt them all their future days.

The wizened old shaman stepped up to the last two men who were fastened to the stakes, the minister Jacob Collins and a farmer named Paterzun, a Dutch settler who had been violently assaulted, his wounds open and weeping blood, but was still defiant. Both men looked at the old Indian with stolid faces.

"You are the examples that will show the power of my dark god to all," Karkuk said. He flashed a thin smile, "Then my followers will know without doubt; for there can be no doubt in them for us to be able to drive away the forces of your iron and steel." He raised his hands above each of the men's heads with his twisted fingers spread in a strange benediction.

He began to mumble in a deep voice. His words were of the most ancient of the Wyandot language but with many words unspoken by any other living of their tribe, secret words, words of power.

After a few moments the two captive men began to moan, and their faces contorted as flaming pain passed through all their bound limbs. They began to vibrate in agony as the magick force visibly rippled through them. The women and children watching began to cry once more with a new level of terror in the tone of their wails.

"Become the symbol of what will happen to of all the white skins! Our land and the spirits will claim all your kind!"

As he spoke a strange change began to come over the two men. Their face contorted to hideous masks of pain and then the color of the skin began to morph and darken. The texture of their flesh began to alter so that in a few minutes the surface of their skin no longer looked like human skin at all; it had the aspect of some gnarled wood with deep ridges and whirls as it darkened and hardened into a bark-like covering.

The two men's moans rose in volume till they became wails to rival the cries of the damned. The women and children's voices stilled as they absorbed the enormity of the abomination that they were seeing. Even the forest seemed to fall silent as the two men screamed their last as living beings and then their voices were stilled forever as their humanity was ended.

After what seemed an eternity the two that had been men were no longer moving and no longer men.

When the wizened old man stepped back from the unmoving forms it was two carved wooden statues stood where they had been, their faces the twisted image of the False Face masks the forest shamans often wore in religious ceremonies.

…their skin no longer looked like human skin…

All the watching native braves shuddered in ecstatic acceptance of the miracle they had witnessed, proof that the man they followed and the gods they worshipped were true and powerful. More powerful than even they had believed before. Now they knew that victory over the white invaders was completely assured.

The little wizard was not done with his display of terror and power, however. He gestured for the braves that held the gathered blood in the cups from the murdered male settlers to come forward.

The Huron surrounded the wizened Karkuk and held their bloody prizes up to the sky in offering.

"Nadie, hear me," the old shaman called to the sky, "I, Karkuk of the Huron call on you to come to me; by the sacrifice of these white invaders, I invoke your protection for myself for our people. And ask a boon: may I fight as once I was and cloak myself in your powerful protection. I ask that no weapon of man, our people or of the invaders be able to harm my form, that you keep me safe: for this I grant you my life in service."

As the shaman spoke the surrounding warriors stepped forward and one by one poured the gory libations over the old man's wizened body. The dark liquid life flowed over his spindly limbs and sunken chest painting him as a dark crimson idol, looking both more and less than human.

The shaman began a chant in the secret and ancient language of the shamans, a low rumbling sound that came from deep within like distant thunder. It came from the very darkest corner of his soul and rolled out of him growing with increasing volume and energy.

The watching warriors took up the chant and soon the valley walls themselves seemed to reverberate with the primordial tones of their supplications. The Hurons summoned the power of their dark and savage god, imploring their leader to call down justice on the white invaders.

"You will pay for this horrible violation of the laws of nature and man," a strong voice from the knot of captive women cut through the musical prayer of the killers, "The God above will not let this sacrilege go unpunished."

The speaker was Deirdre Collins. The wife of Deacon Collins had been roughly treated. Her wimple now askew to free a shock of black hair and her eyes were red rimmed and sunken from her exhausting night. Yet the gaze of the woman was clear and focused like chips of flint on the painted shaman.

While the others around her looked on, the horrors they had witnessed with eyes full of fear or anger her eyes reflected only a certainty of her religion and its tenants. That and fierce independence.

"You will suffer the torments of the damned," she proclaimed as she stood in defiance. "Judgment will flow from the brow of The Lord and wash you away like dirt you are."

One of the Huron stepped in to drive a backhand slap across Dierdre's face that knocked the woman to the ground and opened a cut on her cheek. He was about to strike her again when the voice of the old shaman stopped him.

"Let the white skinned priestess speak," he said with amusement. "The empty words of the invaders have no power in Nadie's realm."

The woman stood and faced the shaman. Her grey eyes blazing with righteous fury. "You will call the wraith of the holy God of his innocent flock upon you…"

"There are no innocents in the realm of the white skins," the shaman said. "The woods and trees, the lakes and rivers, the very land itself is in our hearts and all parts of our being and we are in it. It is ours because we belong to it; you and your people have no respect for it and will all suffer for this when Nadie is fully upon me:" He raised his arms and in the suddenly bright dawn light his gore soaked figure was awesomely horrific.

"Nadie!" he called to the heavens in a voice that suddenly rivaled thunder in volume. "You who were cast into the dark places by the Great Spirit hear me; with these sacrifices I make myself yours!"

As all assembled watched the old man went through a convulsion, his frail, blood drenched body shuddering like a sapling in a strong wind. He began to mumble and foam at the mouth and then, just when it appeared his old body would collapse from the strain of his paroxysms, an astounding change came over him.

The old shaman stood up straight and his wizened body abruptly gained both mass and stature. His leathery skin smoothed out and began to have the supple sheen of youth. Before the startled eyes of all those present the old man became even a more powerful and tall a muscular Huron warrior he had been in his youth.

"Behold the power of the demon-god Nadie," the shaman-warrior's voice now boomed. He addressed his people in English so the captives could appreciate his power. "I am the demon-made man; no weapon of the white skins may harm this shell; I will lead you all in driving the outlanders from our land forever." When he saw the look of bewilderment on the faces of the captive settlers, he smiled a hideous smile.

"Take the whelps and the women to the holy place in Dekanawa," he ordered in his own language. "There we will give them to the darkness of Nadie and all final power will ours—all you, my warriors, will be granted the powers that are now mine only; I will move to destroy the fort at the river ford while you do as I order."

The women and children began to cry as the Huron warriors pulled them to their feet to drive them further into the deep woods. Now the captives moved with their eyes downcast and hopeless. All save Minister Collin's wife who stared directly into the eyes of the transformed magician with malignant hate.

He saw the look and laughed a hideous, demented cackle and then moved off to lead his attack secure in his invincibility and power.

CHAPTER FOUR

TERROR ON THE MOVE...

The village of Kingsborough had grown up around Fort Frontier in the east end of a valley that was a determined finger pointing into the fringes of the forests. It was one of four valleys that cut through the hills and thrust like an inlet into the dense deep woods near the Ohio River, an area which had never been civilized by English settlers.

At the moment the village was a sprawling mess of confused settlers who were unsure as to whether to run into the fort or stay behind the low earthen works barrier that protected the houses from roving animals or casual intrusion. The question on all their minds was, '*how real was the Wyandot threat this time?*'

The settlement fort itself was a madhouse of activity when Declinn raced through the partly closed stockade gate. The King's soldiers, in their red and white uniforms, were marching across the Quadrille and pack horses were being loaded in preparation of an excursion into the wilderness.

"Declinn!" one of the buckskin wearing scouts for the soldiers called to the sculptor. The scout stood with a clot of men that were sitting inside the gate and debating just about everything as they waited for assignments. The scout was grey-haired and leather skinned, and it was clear from his dress and attitude he spent more time in the woods than the settlements.

"Hunkin, you old coot," Declinn greeted. "I thought your scalp was decoration on a Wyandot lodge by now." The two men laid their hands on each other shoulders in a warm friend's greeting.

"I'm too stringy for any of them tree dwellers to want as a souvenir; but up at Willow Creek they say Karkuk's been decorating a lot of lodges."

"Who brought the word in?" Declinn asked his manner remained casual but Hunkin, who knew him and the things that had happened when the tall woodsman had been in Rogers Rangers during the war, sensed a deep emotion. The two friends walked toward the commander's office greeting other woodsmen and settlers who recognized the tall sculptor.

"It was a King's messenger bringing dispatches from the Orin's Ford rode in heading toward Willow Creek right after the feathered devils did the deed;

he spun around and headed straight back here screaming all the way. That was two full days ago."

The two men reached the entrance to the commandant of the fort's office and were stopped by an armed soldier on guard.

"Declinn Blayde," the sculptor said, "The commander called me in."

"Send him in, Sergeant," a voice commanded from within the office. "And Master Hunkin as well." The two men walked past the guard and entered a room thick with the smell of fear and tobacco smoke.

There were just over a dozen men standing around a sand table in the center of a large tactical room. The features of the surrounding region as far west as the Schenectady Basin were molded in relief over a rough map with details being filled in all the time by traders and scouts.

Half of those in the room were the officers from the garrison, the rest were militiamen and town council elders. Most knew Declinn from his scouting activities. All knew Hunkin.

"Master Blayde," the commander of the fort said. Major Arn Macalister was an experienced officer who had campaigned in the old world but who had been on the frontier for less than a year. In that time, however, he had come to respect the opinions of the locals. "Thank you for coming so quickly."

"Quick is the only way when the Indians are on the war trail," Declinn said. "How bad is it?"

"Very bad," a junior officer said. He had an unlined handsome face with brown eyes and light auburn hair that was gathered into a tail in the back by a bright red ribbon. "The devils had set the torch to the whole settlement and killed everyone. They staked them out first."

"Not likely everyone," Declinn suggested.

"I was there…" the young soldier said. "Are you questioning the veracity of an officer of the King?"

"Not your honesty, sir," Declinn said with no rancor. "Just your ability to observe so horrific a scene accurately. I suspect there were only men on the stakes, weren't there?"

The soldier looked at him and for a moment it appeared that he was going to raise an objection, but his commander's voice cut off any outburst.

"Why would you make such an assumption, Mister Blayde?" The senior officer asked.

"The Huron— who you folks often call Wyandot— find great power in the concept of sacrifice," the sculptor explained. "And the women and children would be a powerful medicine if sacrificed."

He stared down at the sand table and traced a finger along the trail from the fort to the razed settlement. "They perform a religious ceremony that is unique to these people that is called the 'Feast of the Dead.' This occurs once every decade." He looked up in the faces of those in the room, men who knew him but who still found much of this tall man a mystery. "At that time the body's of all people who have died over the last ten years were dug up and reburied in a communal burial plot. The Huron believe that this ceremony is necessary to allow the souls of the departed to enter into the spirit realm. That ten years is up around now; if Karkuk makes a sacrifice in one of their sacred groves around now it will be very big medicine for him. And big medicine is what a war leader like Karkuk needs to keep control of his braves going against superiorly armed Crown forces."

"I thought they often took women to their lodges?" The soldier asked.

"A buck might take a particular captive from another tribe as 'war spoils,'' Declinn said, "but aside from thinking our women are too much trouble to be able train on how to live in the woods— less they were taken real young— when the braves are massed in the kind of numbers it took to kill Paterzun and the men up at Willow Creek —no—they would take them as gift to their war god for certain."

"So, we have two problems then," the Major said, "finding the captives if still alive—which Master Blayde says is possible for a time at least—and intercepting this force of Wyandot warriors."

"We have to protect this settlement," one of the older town council members demanded. "We can't send you all off when those devils might come down on our heads."

"I will protect this settlement as I see fit, Mister Buckner," the Major said sharply, "and I am charged by the Crown to pacify this area; both of these tasks will be done as I see fit."

The two older men glared at each other with the others in the room watching them to see who would back down first. It was the local elder who turned his eyes back to the sand table and said, "We can not let our militia traipse off into the deep woods to leave our families unguarded."

"And you shall not," the Major conceded doing his best to be diplomatic. "I will send a reconnaissance force ahead and only move my main force when I am sure I know where the savages are." He turned to a subordinate.

"Captain Cairn, you will take a reconnaissance in force along the road, reinforce Fort Orn at the ford and then move on to track the renegades from the site of Willow Creek."

"If I might suggest, Major," Declinn interjected, "we send a small group of forest runners along the old deer path through the mountains to Willow Creek here—" He pointed to where he had been staring at the map— "we can determine where the Huron went then send someone back down to meet your force at Orn—Four or five runners on this path can cut the triangle— its faster than the road- and meet your force by the time it gets to Orn."

The officer looked at the map, studying it carefully. Fort Frontier and Kingsborough were on the west of a triangle of rough hills. To get to Fort Orn and beyond it to the furthest settlement out in the wilderness, Willow Creek the relief force would have to march south to where the spur road joined the one to Fort Orn before marching north again. The forest path that the sculptor indicated cut through a narrow pass through the hills that went directly northeast.

"That could put the runners in harms way directly, Master Blayde," the officer said.

"We are all in harms way, sir, if we don't know where the Huron force is; besides, if we take woodsmen we should know enough to avoid running directly into the middle of any red shenanigans."

The officer considered for a moment and then nodded. "It is a good plan—but take Lieutenant Bonny." He indicated the young messenger who had brought the news of the massacre and had spoken up earlier. "I wish there to be Crown presence at the site of the slaughter as soon as possible."

The young officer looked a little aghast at the suggestion but was disciplined enough to say nothing.

"We had better start as soon as possible," Declinn said. "We can get well into the mountains by dark and travel with the full moon for part of the night."

"Pick your five, Master Blayde," the Major agreed, "and take what stores you will need from the quartermaster. Go with him, Lieutenant and good luck."

The young man saluted and followed the sculptor and Hunkin out of the room.

"You head with the soldier boys," Declinn said to the other buckskin clad forester. "You can't run worth spit on that old knee of yours and we need somebody to keep those fool redcoats from drowning themselves fording the river."

The older woodsman spit some chewing tobacco out and nodded. "'Bout how I saw it to. I'll make sure we're at Orn when you show up. I'll go get the boys from the pub and send the runners over to you at the storage house. Stop by for a drink before you head out." He waved off and headed across the quadrangle to where the militia were milling about.

"Can you run, Lieutenant?" Declinn asked as the two walked to across the busy main yard toward the storehouse.

"I will not slow you down," the young man said. He came just to the shoulder of the muscular woodsman and his pale skin was a contrast to the sun bronzed skin of the colonial. "I can keep a good pace."

"Not in those boots, I am afraid" Declinn said. "They are good for riding, but you'll be crippled inside of an hour on the trail. See if the storeroom has any buckskin boots that fit."

"I am a uniformed officer of the Crown, Master Blayde—"

"Declinn's good for anyone but the Major—I've had a year and can't get him to call me by my right name."

"Master Declinn." The officer objected, "I am under the orders of my commanding officer; not colonials."

"Ain't giving you orders, Lieutenant, just making a suggestion." The woodsman clarified. "I never tell a man what to do; nature and experience are much more instructive than I'll ever be." Before the younger man could react to the statement the frontiersman had entered the storeroom and held the door open. The soldiers hesitated.

"Whatever you decide, Lieutenant," Declinn continued, "do it quickly, I want to be heading up the trail in fifteen minutes. We have a date with some hair-lifters and I don't want to keep them waiting."

CHAPTER FIVE

INTO THE VALLEY OF THE SHADOW

The group of five woodsmen and Lieutenant Bonny, the Crown officer (wearing buckskin boots) took off in a little over twenty minutes from when they received their charge to race to the burning settlement of Willow Creek.

They went out from the palisade of Fort Frontier at a relaxed trot. The men moved in single file and left the defined trail less than a hundred yards from the town line to take off cross country.

All the men wore light packs and carried long rifles save for Lieutenant Bonny who carried a Crown issue Brown Bess musket and Declinn who also carried a bow and arrow. "Sometimes we want to not advertise where we are," the sculptor told Bonny when the soldier questioned his choice. "And I can send half a dozen of these shafts while most are sending three musket balls out."

After picking their way through the brush for a slow two miles the group emerged onto the deer path that the woodsmen knew of and began to make good time heading to the Northeast through a narrow pass in the mountains toward Willow Creek.

Declinn stayed out front for most of the day, his long-legged stride and powerful lungs setting a brisk pace. His goal was to make it well into the hills by nightfall. The British officer found himself pushing himself to his own limits to keep up with the colonials though he did his best not to acknowledge it. He was delighted when, as twilight came over the deep woods, the line of runners called a halt and fell off to the side off the trail to rest.

Declinn was running just ahead of the Englishman at that point so the two ended up resting in a hollow beside the trail that had been made by the fall of a storm-uprooted tree.

"Drink?" the woodsman handed his companion a waterskin. The officer took the libation and gulped down two mouth fulls.

"Thank you," the officer said. "I thought we were going to run most of the night?" He was pale and out of breath but still kept his uniform jacket buttoned up to this collar. He sat upright against the fallen tree's trunk thankful for the solid rest.

"That's the plan," Declinn said. The woodsman seemed as fresh as when they had started the run. He removed his dark green buckskin jacket and hung it inside out on a branch then gathered some fallen leaves into a makeshift sleeping pallet. "But we have a couple of hours until moonrise so now's the time to get some solid rest; we'll push hard when the moon is up, and we can see better. Then with moon-fall we'll take another short sleep." With that he rolled over and, with the true forest dweller's ability to rest on command, was soon snoring beside the startled officer.

It took the junior officer quite a while to find a comfortable position for his aching muscles. He found the prospect of sleeping on the ground in the middle of what he considered a hostile environment hard to deal with, but his exhaustion won over his reluctance, and he soon slept soundly.

In what seemed like only moments Lieutenant Bonny was being shaken awake by the woodsman-sculptor.

"Time to move, Lieutenant," Declinn prompted. "Moon's just up and a clear night. it's good and bright, easy to see."

It was. The dark pathways of the forest were illuminated in blue-white light that gave it a ghostly look but was bright and clear enough to keep them from breaking an ankle as they jogged along.

"Here; grab a chew." Blayde handed the groggy officer a small ball of food wrapped in a broad leaf. When the solider looked at it oddly the sculptor explained. "Its pemmican; mix of nuts and jerky and wild rice that the Indians use for a quick energy boost when they need it. It's a bit on the chewy side, but it'll do the job and sticks to your ribs well enough to keep you going."

The officer took it with skepticism evident on his face but after two bites his hunger took over and he wolfed it down.

"Yep, it does the job," Declinn laughed, "and after two days on the trail it will taste better than venison steak."

"I think that will take a few more than two days on the trail for that," the

Englishman said with a genial smile, "but it does make me feel a bit more energetic."

The seven runners moved at a good pace, not fully the speed they had during the day, but not much less either. There was no conversation, and no need for it. Each man knew the dangers they were running toward and the risks they were taking in doing it, but they also knew the consequences if they ignored the threat or shirked their duty. The future of settlements in the entire Mohawk Valley and possibly of European settlement in the new continent were at stake. And the lives of all their friends and families.

The French to the north favored only limited settlement, which was why they had secured the aid of so many Indian tribes; they wanted only the fur trade and other limited raw resources. It was the British who sent wholesale colonies and treated any natives they found as mere obstacles to the British agenda rather than human beings with their own rights and ways. It was deliberate racial arrogance and ruthlessness carried out with practiced ease and callous force.

Blayde stayed in the forefront of the group with easy, distance eating strides, his features neutral, but his thoughts were not so placid. His mind went back to a time during the war when he had also raced against great odds and the sands of time to carry a warning, but then he had been too late; he carried a rock of fear in his soul he might be again. Even the knife wound in his shoulder, long healed, throbbed with the memory and guilt of his failure. He prayed hard he would not be. He could not be—this time it was too important and far too personal.

The group of scouts ran until the moon was almost gone behind the horizon and then, just when Bonny felt he could not take another step, bedded down again for a longer sleep 'til dawn. This time the junior officer had no misgivings at all, his exhaustion washing any hesitation from his mind so that he slept as quickly and deeply as the woodsmen he ran with and with whom he was coming to admire.

The dawn was a wet one with a light rain falling, the mists swirling through the deep forest imparting an eerie unreality to the woods. The group was forced to move more slowly because of the wet conditions but within an hour of sun-up the warming rays soon penetrated even the closely packed trees drying the trail and warming the men. It almost became a pleasant run when they reached the gentle upward slope that told them they were near the valley that held the Willow Creek settlement.

The group struck off the deer path once they were through the mountains and were soon within sight of the ridge beyond which they knew the Willow Creek Village was located. Then the men slowed, proceeding with caution as they approached the sight of the massacre, weapons at the ready, eyes scanning and all senses alert.

The land was still.

No animals moved. No insect skittered. No birds sang in the trees.

The smoke from the still smoldering buildings drifted over the ridge above the valley adding a nightmarish quality to the whole scene. The horror of it all added solemnity to the movements of the seven as they descended from the pass along the deer trail.

The scout party proceeded through the smoke as it crawled up the hills toward them like a living thing. It had a vague scent of destruction and death about it, a charred stench that became oppressive as it enveloped them. It made them all uneasy so that none spoke.

The woodsmen were all hardened men, who had endured much just to live in the wild country they called home, but their gorge's still rose with the smell and the sight of their friends and neighbors slaughtered like animals. The bodies of the bloodless men hung limp on the line of stakes. The scavengers had already been at some of the corpses, tearing chunks from the tender, exsanguinated flesh, which added to the hellishness of the scene.

"They had no chance," Lieutenant Bonny gasped. His voice was a hoarse whisper and there were tears in his eyes. His hands, gripping his rifle shook with suppressed rage.

The sculptor stood by his side and silently took in the scene with narrowed eyes. His shoulders hunched with his own internalized anger, but his face stayed impassive though he clenched his jaw. When the soldier made a move to cut down the first of the slaughtered villagers Declinn put a restraining hand on his arm.

"No, we had better leave them for the present, Lieutenant."

"But we have to give them a Christian burial!"

"And we will, later," the sculptor said quietly. "We can't risk a scouting party of Huron discovering we've been here if we do anything to change this: remember we have to find the others if we can, that is more important. I'm sure the Lord above will understand a little delay in sending them on officially with all the trimmings.

"But—" he soldier gasped, then added, "Yes, I suppose they..."

"Here!" One of the woodsmen called with a strangled tone. He was kneeling at the end of the line of staked victims. "Fellas, you have to see this!"

The group of scouts all moved to the end of the line of bodies to see the remains of the two settlers that had been ensorcelled. Their transformed bodies were frozen in the last moments of horrid torment, their features contorted in perpetual twisted agony. It appeared as if their bodies had been sculpted, changed entirely into roughhewn wooden forms.

This new horror was almost overwhelming for the men. They stood stunned beyond words for many minutes with more than one man saying a silent prayer.

"Could they be—some sort of carved fetish?" The Englishman ventured haltingly. "Idols or statues of some sort?"

Declinn stepped forward and despite his revulsion touched a hand to the cheek of figure of the transformed Minister Collins. His knowing fingers caressed the face of the gnarled figure with reverence.

"This is—or was, Deacon Jacob Collins," Declinn said. His sculptor's eyes appraised the shape before him. "No human hand made this contour." He turned to look at his companions, "This is some sort of black magick; this is the work of that devil from the deep woods."

"Karkuk," one of the woodsmen muttered but all the woodsmen knew it must be so.

"How in all that is holy do we fight this?" Bonny asked.

"With all we have," Declinn with a quiet determination in his voice. "Until we can't fight any more and then we start again. We fight this until five minutes after we are dead." He turned to the others his hand still in contact with the death mask of the minister. "Now we have to find those women and children and the black magic devil that did this."

The woodsmen scattered then and moved to the edges of the clearing to locate some sign of the Hurons and their captives.

It did not take long until they found clear trace of their passage.

"They weren't even trying to hide their trail," one of the woodsmen said as he looked at the trampled grass and broken bushes that showed which way the huddled mass of prisoners had gone.

"The women and children went this way with a small force of braves," a rail thin man with blond hair and a full beard spoke. His quiet voice was full of rage. "All in a tight group—probably roped together. And yes, there was no attempt to hide their trail; the Hurons were pretty sure no white man would ever get this far." He looked up at the tall sculptor looking for guidance for the next move.

"Here's why, Grover," Declinn called out from where he crouched studying the ground, "The main body of the Hurons headed down the trail toward Fort Orn." He was kneeling, his nose almost pressed into the dirt, his keen eyes studying every blade of grass. "Been long gone enough that they could already be at the fort I suspect."

"Why didn't I run into them when I rode in with the dispatches?" Lieutenant Bonny asked. "I came up that road and went right back down it—the buildings were still burning hot when I got to the top of the ridge here."

"They must have had scouts out and saw you coming so they hid from you; one man would not have been a threat, but they could use you as a way to get the word quickly to Kingsborough. This was all about luring the garrison to Orn and away from Kingsborough," Declinn reasoned. "That means they can tie up troops at the fort and the settlement will then be vulnerable."

"The major outsmarted them then," Bonny said, "by only sending a strong reconnaissance force."

"They'll still be overwhelmed by the numbers these tracks indicate." One of the other woodsmen countered. He was as burly as Declinn but shaped more like an ale keg with close cropped red-haired. "Unless they are able to fight their way into the fort."

"We have to warn them then." the officer looked around in an agitated state as if he would find an answer to this new dilemma in the edge of the woods.

"We can't do anything for the force at Fort Orn," Declinn said, "but we can warn Kingsborough and tell the Major what we suspect."

"They used me to bait their trap?" the junior officer's voice became shrill. "I'm responsible for those men being in danger!"

"Anyone who came in at that point would have been used," Declinn said. "You could just as easily have been on one of those staked out over here, no reason to blame yourself, Lieutenant. Things just work out that way sometimes."

"I would rather have been that then be responsible for leading my men to destruction!"

The tall sculptor made a disgusted sound. "Oh, stop it; you're wasting time, man. I know something about guilt, and I can tell you it does no good. There are women and children who need out help; we can pity ourselves when we have saved them."

The officer looked daggers at the sculptor but then swallowed and nodded. "Correct, sir, forgive my indulgence."

"Okay, Josiah," Declinn turned to another of the woodsmen, "You're the fastest of us all, hightail it back to Kingsborough and let them know what's going on. We're going after the women folk 'cept for Grover." He looked over at the bearded forester. "I figure you're sneaky enough to maybe make it to Fort Orn and sneak around it, just in case there's a chance to warn the boys that are on the way from Kingsborough."

"None sneakier," the thin woodsman chuckled. "Be seein' you all; hold on to your hair." He turned and trotted down the trail with no more ceremony. He was soon lost around a bend in the trail.

"Same for me," Josiah called with a grim smile as he trotted off back the way they had come.

Lieutenant Bonny watched them both leave, marveling at the way the woodsmen seemed to function as if they had a hierarchy and as equals all at once; they seemed to sense what had to be done like a hive mind and acted with no sense of inferiority to do whatever job they were best suited for.

"You comin', Lieutenant?" Declinn asked as he and the remaining three men started up the trail after the victims. "We still have a job to do."

"Yes, sir," Bonny said aloud, "We certainly do." And then he took off at a trot after the others, deeper into the foreboding wall of the dense woods, somehow feeling not so hopeless as moments before.

CHAPTER SIX

DOORWAY TO HELL!

The remaining five of the scouting party followed the trial of the Huron warriors and their prisoners until it became too dark to track, but by then Declinn had surmised where they were headed.

"Dekanawa," he said, "a holy ground where they bury their chiefs on the shore of Scanada Lake; they have to be headed there for sure from these tracks."

"They can't move fast with the women and kids," Conners, a redhead with a long scar on his left cheek said. "Even with a two-day head start we can catch them up."

"Yes," Declinn said. "If we keep going." He looked at the officer, resting on a tree stump. "We'll take ten and then move out; you up for it, Lieutenant?"

The officer looked up from massaging a sore ankle and gave a slight smile. "A whole ten minutes?" He said, "Are you getting soft, Mister Declinn?"

"Could be," the sculptor said with an answering grin, "Lots of people say that about me these days." He sat down next to the Englishman and took a drink of water, offering the skin to the younger man.

After a few moments, and not being really aware of it, Declinn picked up a piece of wood, drew his belt knife and began to whittle at the stick.

"Is that what you do?" Bonny asked.

"What?"

"Carve with a knife," the soldier said. "I know I've heard talk around the settlement that you're supposed to be quite a sculptor." Declinn snorted.

"Supposed to be?"

"No offense meant. I just would never have thought a—I mean a fellow out here in the woods who makes cupids and all that."

This time the woodsman's laugh was full-chested. "I haven't made a cupid yet, and I usually use these tools—" he produced one of his chisels from his sidepack, holding it up like a proud father with a favorite child. "I don't have an explanation for it either. Its just something I've always done; some folk look at a patch of land and see a farm, I look at a piece of wood and see a critter or a person." He held up the stick he had been carving, and the head of a snake was already beginning to emerge from the end of it, roughly shaped, but clearly visible in the fading light.

"I'm a third-generation soldier," Lieutenant Bonny said. "But sometimes I think it would be good to create something instead of—well—only be a destroyer; be it a farm from the wilderness or a statue of a Cupid from a tree."

Declinn handed the stick-snake to the young man. "You soldiers helped us to create the settlement's, Lieutenant, that is not at all about destroying. Every man has his purpose under the heavens. Never sell yourself short if you do the best you can; be proud of what you do. The world needs, farmers and fishermen, weavers, farriers and cavalry just as much. At least until all men can learn to live in peace. And that means red and white and black as well." He stood up. "And so, far as I can tell you're as good a soldier as they get, and so far, turning into a pretty fair woodsman as well."

The officer stood up and stretched. "Nice of you to say so, sir but how would you know?"

"Well, at least I know you can run like a colonial, and that's good enough for me."

The others were on their feet as well and without another word the four of them began to move off at a cautious walk, navigating by the stars.

When the moon rose, they made better speed though the going was rough and even though they twice they lost it was obvious trail the prisoners were leaving for them. The Huron captors had not even bothered to try and hide any trace of their passage, arrogantly sure that no one would be following them.

Just after dawn the five exhausted men broke through the undergrowth of the deep woods to a gently sloping meadow that led to a broad lake. On the shore of the lake the cluster of the women and children could be seen seated on the ground. There were five braves standing around them facing out toward the lake.

Declinn pointed beyond the prisoners to an island in the center of the lake where figures could be seen moving about. "That's where the medicine place is," he said. "The main force must be out there; I reckon they did not have enough canoes to bring all the prisoners across at once."

"We might get the guards here," Bonny said, "but they'll be off the island and upon us in no time."

"Sure enough," Declinn fitted an arrow to his bow, holding three more between the fingers of his left hand. "But we'll never have a better chance to get those women and young ones free." The other three woodsmen had already moved out to flank the group on the shore of the lake with no verbal

"Is that what you do?"

order having been given.

The officer watched the three men move into position, amazed that they all knew what must be done and how to do it. "You all work as one," his whispered. "It still amazes me."

"We just know what has to be done," the woodsman whispered as he focused ahead to the battle to come. "I'll let them get as close as they can before I let loose with the arrows. We'll avoid using the rifles and we might have a chance of getting a head start with the town's folk before those on the island know we were here."

The officer nodded and the two of them crept through the tall grass of the meadow toward the prisoners. They moved silently and quietly, holding their breaths, eyes focused on the distracted Indian guards, hoping they would not look back at the prisoners.

After all the woodsmen were in place, as close to the prisoners as possible with cover, there was a whistling sound, and a tomahawk flew over the heads of the villagers and thudded into the back of one of the Hurons near the lake shore.

This was signal for Declinn to rise and fire four arrows as fast as he could draw the bow. It was so rapid that the eye could not follow the shafts as he launched them.

Each shaft slammed into the back of one of the Indian guards. One of the Huron did not fall from the arrow though and spun to try and face his attacker. He began to open his mouth to scream an alarm but one of the colonial woodsmen rose out of the grass near him and leapt forward to tackle him. The white scout made quick and silent work of the Huron warrior with a knife.

The woodsmen all rose and raced to the prisoners to keep them from making any noise, at the same time pulling the dead Indians from the water's edge to hide them.

Lieutenant Bonny was amazed at how quickly the women and children, so ready to celebrate salvation were quieted with the understanding of the need for stealth. Even the youngest of the children, barely out of diapers, had the discipline of the frontier raised and were up and ready in moments.

The woodsmen gathered up the weapons from the fallen Huron and handed two of the rifles and powder horns to women who they knew could use them.

"Thank God in his mercy, Declinn!" the Widow Collins murmured as the woodsman and the soldier moved in among the prisoners. She threw her arms around the tall woodsman and allowed her strength to soften for a moment.

"How're you holding up, sis?" Declinn asked.

She fought back tears and stepped away from the sculptor. "Fine," she said, "but that monster Karkuk is the devil himself. He claims no weapon of man can harm him and I'm afraid he might be right. He's an evil sorcerer charged with the dark one's powers."

"I know," the woodsman said. "I saw what he did to Jacob. I'm truly sorry; he was a good man."

"Yes," she said in a graveyard echo. "My husband was a very good man."

Bonny could see the resemblance of the woodsman and the widow, piercing eyes and a strong jawline and a certain inner strength of character that made the Englishman think that there must be something special in the air of the colony. It seemed to put steel it put into the spines of all its inhabitants, even the young ones.

The group of women and children were all exhausted from the long hard march through the woods. Nevertheless they mobilized quickly and began to move back toward the way they had come when the scouts prompted them.

Lieutenant Bonny grabbed Declinn's arm and pulled him aside.

"You'll need someone to cover your rearguard," the officer said to the sculptor. "The best chance to bottle them up is here. If one were to snipe at them as they cross from that island one man with several rifles could hold them back for a good, long while." The taller man regarded the officer for a long moment.

"I'd planned to take up that little chore myself," Declinn said quietly. "I figure it's my right."

"I've seen the way you do things out here in the woods, sir," the officer said, "You don't command; you all do what has to be done because you understand what works best. Well— I am nowhere near the woodsmen any of you are. What I am is a good marksman. At least I can shoot well enough to hold them off for a good enough amount of time to matter. I can load and fire three shots in a minute easily, even under fire."

"They're not likely to take kindly to be sniped at."

"And if anything goes wrong on the trail back, you and your men can deal with it better than I." The officer straightened his collar and dusted off his jacket, pulling himself to attention. "You make your cupids, Mister Declinn and I will do what I do. At least this way I can create an opportunity for escape."

The woodsman nodded. "You'll need another powder horn and two of those long rifles from the Hurons; they have a bit more range than your musket." One of the other woodsmen brought powder horns and rifles when summoned. And he handed the officer a small flask as well.

"Store bought corn," the colonial said with a ghost of a smile, "has a bite but does the job."

"I hope I can say the same for myself," the officer said as he took a parting swig.

"I think you can," Declinn said, putting a hand on his shoulder and nodded a silent benediction. Then the frontiersman he turned to head off with the prisoners, adding, "Like I said, you're as good a soldier as they get, been an honor to run with you."

CHAPTER SEVEN

SUMMONING THE DARK

Lieutenant Bryan Bonny lay prone behind a fallen log on the shore of the lake. Two powder horns, the shot for half a dozen volleys and two long rifles set beside him. He had the Brown Bess musket set back behind him for the closer work when the time came.

He could not load and fire the colonial long weapons as quickly as his own shorter weapon, but the long rifles gave him not only distance but a rifled shot that would be accurate in sniping at the Huron all the way to those on the island.

The Brown Bess was meant to be a volley weapon for His Majesty's forces, since training the army was always geared to mass engagements, with the exception of certain chosen men designated as snipers. Still, the Bess would do the job for close work and when time came the officer knew he could load and fire own weapon faster with an old friend's familiarity. He had no illusion but that he would not have to get off all that many shots before he fell, but he did know he would make the Huron pay dearly for his scalp!

Bonny studied the shore of the distant island but could see no sign for a time that the freeing of the prisoners had even been noticed. There were canoes lined up on the open beach with no cover for any who might be defending the island for some distance across the sandy expanse. That would work in his favor.

He tried not to dwell on the chances of the prisoners, as he pictured in his mind's eye that they were fleeing down the forest paths. He knew they would move as swiftly as possible, but in fact, even with their iron constitutions, after the ordeal they had been through that was not so very fast at all.

Bonny gave no thought to escaping himself, of ever meeting up with them again. He thought instead of his upbringing in Derbyshire and of the horse farm his father, who was injured out of the service, had managed. His father had been able to save enough to put his only son in the best schools and purchased Bryan's commission in the army. Bonny had known from the start that was what he wanted and looked forward to a long and honorable career. Something to make his father proud.

Not so long, he thought with a wry smile. *But I hope this will make you proud, father.* He was surprised there was no fear in him, no dread of what might come, only a calm understanding of what must be done to give the women and children a chance.

This must be what the colonials feel, seeing the whole picture and knowing their place in it. For a soldier who had been trained to see only his small part in an operation this sudden understanding that he was a vital part of a whole filled him with a contentment and real purpose. That understanding allowed him to wait calmly, scanning the shore of the island with a steady gaze.

It was a full half hour before the island showed activity and the figures that congregated on the beach began to notice that their sentinels on the shore were not visible. A few of the Huron warriors on the beach began to gesture and point in the direction of the shore, generally pointing near the soldier's position. When the Indian began to push a canoe into the water to start across, he leveled a long rifle and sighted.

"At least," he reasoned out loud to no one in particular, "My *short* career will have a spectacular and honorable end."

+++

The survivors of Willow Creek Settlement moved with the stoic determination of people who had pitted themselves against the wilderness as a daily course of life and refused to be defeated. Despite the hardships they had endured even the children knew that there was no alternative than to press on and so there were no complaints even when Declinn and the three woodsmen exhorted them to move more quickly.

The prisoners were not trying to delay the Hurons now as they had when being brought toward the sacred island. Now they were moving toward freedom and salvation, so they found the inner strength to press on gaining some speed.

The group had traveled for almost an hour when they heard the first gunshots behind them from the lake. They all paused for a moment, their thoughts going back to the shore of the lake, and the sacrifice of the brave man who had stayed behind them there. All crossed themselves then said a silent prayer before moving on, quickening their pace.

"How long do you think that young man will be able to hold out?" Deirdre Collins asked her brother in a quiet whisper. She was as taciturn as her sibling, her jaw set, her head held high despite her exhaustion.

"If he is a fast reloader and a good shot—as he said he was, and I think he probably is—" Declinn said flatly, "maybe an hour before they figure out that he's only one man and they get around him somehow. Fortunately, most of the Huron don't swim to well and that lake is deep."

"I will pray for him," she said as she made the sign of the cross "We all will."

"While you're at it pray for ourselves," he added, "We will need Providence's hand if we're to make it back to Kingsborough with our skins whole."

+++

Bonny waited for the first canoe to make it halfway to the mainland shore before he fired on the lead oarsman. The lead Indian flew back into the canoe and upset it. The Englishman fired again before the rowers fully realized what had happened and killed two more braves with a lucky single rifle ball that passed through both men's heads. A fourth Huron could obviously not swim and after screams and struggles disappeared beneath the limb-numbing cold surface of the water.

The braves that remained on the island took cover and opened up in volley fire in the general direction of Bonny but without a specific target they had no real effect. The English officer moved his position for each new shot following the forest tactics of the colonials.

Also working in his favor was the fact that the distance was almost too great for the Indian's rifles since they were firing slightly uphill to the shore. Many of their musket balls dropped harmlessly into the water. It added to the Huron's distress that to reach the canoes they had to cross an open beach, and he had a clear range of fire for the whole area; *it's almost too easy,* Bonny thought after a time.

The Huron warriors then tried to launch two canoes at once at a spaced distance, but Bonny was able, by racing to different preset positions to rake the craft with deadly accurate fire that killed one in each canoe which caused the survivors to turn back. From the intensity of the return fire, he was sure he had convinced them there was more than one individual firing at them. That made him smile at the deception.

Next the Hurons tried to float logs into the lake and hide behind them but again he was able to shoot the swimmers by shifting positions since he was slightly higher than the surface of the lake and firing down at them.

The British officer kept vigilant and was able to stop several more attempts to cross but he knew it was only a matter of time. He knew the women and children could use every minute he could give them but recognized the reality that they could only move so fast. And he knew his luck would only hold out only so long. There had been an hourglass with the sand running out on him from the very beginning.

Bonny was calmer than he thought he should be, though his muscles were taunt the entire time. His eyes sore from staring so intently across the glare of the lake surface and he feared the strain would take him before any of the Huron did. In any case, even if by some miracle he held out until nightfall, darkness would mean his advantage would be gone.

He smiled. *Well, if I make it as long as sunset, we'll just see how fast this foot soldier can run!*

But, of course, that was just a jest with himself, for almost two hours after his shoreline siege began and a full three after the prisoners had escaped, Bonny's luck ran out.

Several of the Huron made it to shore somewhere up the lake by swimming or holding onto a log then doubled back through the underbrush. They set upon the officer from behind while he was firing on another frontal assault from the island.

Bonny was reloading a long rifle when four of the warriors sprang on him from the landward side, he heard them at the last moment and spun. He managed to fire while the tamping rod was still in the barrel. He put that through the stomach of one attacker, then, grabbed his Brown Bess musket and was quickly able to get one last shot off. This final shot killed a second one of the braves before the other two bore him to the ground by main strength.

Bonny fought with all his might, but one brave struck him a glancing blow with a war club and dazed him. This allowed them to bind him before he was fully awake then they put him in a canoe to transport back to the island.

"You have defied me and stolen the sacrifice that Nadie requires," the broad chested Karkuk growled when he was sure that the new captive was fully conscious. The shaman warrior was furious to discover his plans had been thwarted by a single white man! "So, you will have to be a token of the gifts we will bring to the Dark One when we re-capture the women."

The officer stared in amazement at the hugely powerful shaman. He clearly stood apart from the other Huron, both by his height at over six feet and the raw force that emanated from him. His eyes were black pools of swirling energy. He spoke in English and Bonny was aware that he was doing so for the benefit of the Englishman— to increase the prisoner's terror.

The officer retained an icy calm, however. Even though the actual presence of the savage shaman was almost overwhelming, he had prepared himself to be tortured and killed. Knowing he had given the prisoners the best chance possible bolstered his confidence, and his faith in his God assured he was not shaken.

What happened next did shake his confidence and, indeed, his very belief system as a Godfearing Christian.

"Bring him to the place of summoning," the Shaman Karkuk ordered.

Bonny's bonds were cut, he was seized by six Indians and hoisted to a rough stone alter. It had been carved from the raw rock of an outcropping on a small rise in the center of the sacred island.

There his arms and legs were secured again to the four corners of the slab by rawhide thongs.

"Now you will see the gifts that Nadie has given to me," The shaman proclaimed in a near whisper. "It is my destiny and mission to drive you white-skins from our land." He leaned in to fix his powerful eyes on the prisoner's, holding Bonny's gaze like a snake with a victim. "English and French invaders will both be driven back into the sea or put to the tomahawk to send you all to the darkest of your white god's hells."

"You speak a lot, old fellow," Bonny said in as casual voice as he could muster. "But you say very little." He forced his mouth into a sneer, calling on his memory of a particular Colour-Sergeant who had a certain skill at putting the troops in their place.

The Huron leader's reaction was to laugh. His followers picked up the sound and soon the clearing was awash with the sound of hideous laughter. For some reason that scared the captive more than anything so far in his ordeal.

"I will show you why you will all be driven from this land," the shaman said. "It will be the last thing you will see." He stepped back from the altar and produced a steel bladed knife, raised it to the heavens and, to the shock of the bound officer, in one swift movement, plunged the blade into his own chest. Or at least he attempted to.

When the blade struck the shaman's breast over this heart the point stopped as if it had collided with a solid wall. The Huron shaman repeated the process several times each with enough force that there could be no doubt of trickery or mime— the point was being driven into him with enough force that it would have penetrated the skin of any other man.

To punctuate the gesture, Karkuk raised the blade and drove it into the stone of the altar beside the head of the prisoner. The point chipped and sparks flew. All the Huron cheered as the blade clicked on the stone.

"Nadie has made it so that no weapon of Huron, Iroquois, French or English may harm me." The shaman said, "You and your people are doomed."

The Indian shaman raised his arms in invocation and began to mumble in his native tongue. The other natives fell reverently silent as the prayers were chanted and Bonny was suddenly filled with a horror of the unspeakable and unimaginable thing he had seen.

Bonny remembered the horrid statue-like forms of the two men at the settlement and image filled him with dread of the dark magicks of the Indian. The Englishman began to pray, closing his eyes in an attempt to blot the image of his circumstance from his mind. He tried to picture his home, imagined the cool fall breezes of his youth. He tried to recall the words of a church hymn to blot out the chanting, but it was no use.

The voice of the chanting holy man called Bonny from the darkness of his closed eyes and when he opened them the shaman had changed in a horrid way. The Huron leader was aglow with an inner luminescence, the golden color of the sun reflected off a lake surface. The glow was magnified from the power that coursed from within him and almost made it hard to look directly at Kurkak.

The shaman's eyes, however, were a focused directly on the captive in both challenge and triumph. The inner flames of those dark eyes held the Englishman's gaze as a hawk held a field mouse.

Bonny tried to take his eyes away from the stare, tried to even close them but it was if his body had surrendered control to the savage sorcerer. He fought to turn his head away but the muscles in his neck would not respond to his conscious control.

The officer's breaths became shallow and labored as if there were a weight on his chest, as if some demon of medieval times were perched over his heart and breathing fetid breath into his nostrils.

Bonny tried to push the fancy of the demon image from his mind, but he felt other things as well: a chill up his spine and muscle twitched in his legs and arms. He fought to contract his arms and pull on the ties that bound him, but the limbs had also turned traitor.

"Surrender to the power of the Dark One, Nadie," Karkuk said in English to the soldier. "He will take you to the underworld so that we The People will once more be true masters of our land."

The words were soon meaningless to the captive as the power of the shaman took control of his body. Bonny's ears began to ring, and his throat tightened. He fought to gasp air, but it tasted bitter and metallic. His eyes began to water and his limbs twitched so violent that he appeared to be vibrating on the altar.

The bonds on his limbs were pulled taunt and as he convulsed. The spasm had the effect twisting his body first one way than the other as his arms and legs tightened alternately.

The Huron warriors that stood around the sacred sight were hushed by the spectacle they were witnessing. Many of them, fearless in any battle against any natural odds, felt a cold chill as they watched the sorcery before them. The dark forces their leader was summoning were not an enemy they could ever face or truly understand. It not only reinforced their beliefs but filled them with terror at their insignificance in the cosmos.

Many of them were sure the Great Spirit himself, a creature of the light they were sure would turn away from the shadows being cast that day by the shaman. Yet Karkuk was a leader who had demonstrated he had the power to drive out the British and the French. Their hate of white invaders was far greater than the warriors' terror at the spectacle they had witnessed. They were willing to align with the dark forces to gain their ends.

Lieutenant Bonny felt a warm tingling sensation moving from his outer limbs and slowly crawled though his nerves and muscle fibers toward the trunk of his body. It was like his limbs were simultaneously falling asleep and burning at the same time. The feeling grew in intensity until it became painful, then agonizing.

"God!" Bonny screamed as a particularly violent convulsion wracked his body.

"Yes, Englishman," Karkuk said. "But which God do you call upon? Your white God is far across the water and cannot hear you. Only Nadie the Wise will hear your cries, and he has only one fate in store for you, to be the symbol of the land and of your surrender to it. Give up hope and surrender to the fate that awaits all whites."

The words were distant now to Lieutenant Bryan Bonny who was lost in his own world of pain and disorientation. The afternoon sky and the green horizon began to spin, a kaleidoscope of color and cacophony of discordant sound.

Bonny managed to raise his head to look down his body and was stunned to see that there were changes occurring visually to his lower body as well as inside him. The brown of the buckskin boots was darkening and transforming. The texture of them was changing, becoming rougher and coarser.

His white trousers were transforming as well, assuming the same gnarled texture and color as the boots. And he knew that inside those boots and trousers his body was transforming as well.

He was becoming what he had seen on those stakes at the settlement at Willow Creek. He knew it with a certainty that chilled him to his soul. He could feel each fiber of his being changing, transforming into a twisted image of hell on earth.

The shaman took the knife he had used to stab himself to slash the ropes that secured Lieutenant Bonny to the altar. The twitching officer commanded himself to move and make a run for it only to discover he was able to roll off the stone slab.

The Englishman felt himself compelled by an unspoken order from the shaman to stand upright and came to attention beside the altar.

The old-young shaman assumed a pose like a European soldier and touched his right hand to his forehead in a mock salute. This brought roars of laughter from the watching Huron warriors.

Lieutenant Bonny, his vision fading, his head pounding with agony, fought his own body as the dark magick of the Huron God overwhelmed him. He knew he was doomed, that his life was over and hoped he had delayed the enemy enough to make his death have true value.

As darkness engulfed him the English officer made one last gesture of defiance, forcing by sheer force of will his right hand to touch the back of it to his forehead in a salute. There his hand froze as the final changes came over him.

His last thought before the final dark came over him was, *God save the King and God help Declinn to stop this evil monster,* but he feared that there was no hope against so powerful a sorcerer like the evil incarnate that was Karkuk.

Then the living breathing man that had been Lieutenant Bryan Bonny was completely replaced by the roughhewn statue of a king's messenger frozen in a salute from beyond the grave.

+++

The survivors of Willow Creek Settlement emerged from the woods to the still smoldering sight of their former home exhausted and numbed from the horrors they had seen. Even the children had no more tears when they came in sight of the blackened buildings and the slaughtered men still hanging on the stakes.

Declinn Blayde was holding two children, one in his arms and one on his back and even his indefatigable stride had slowed after the pace he had set through the woods.

"We can't keep going, Dec—" his sister said as she collapsed into the lea of a wide tree. "If we don't rest for a while some of us will drop for good, they just can't keep going."

The sculptor set the two children down by the creek that gave the village its name and along with most of the refugees set to drinking from the fast-moving water.

"We can maybe spare half an hour," Declinn said as he looked back down the trail the way they had come, "But I doubt we can risk much more."

"We just can't do it," she said, "Look at everyone; they are all used up."

He looked around at the grey faces of the women and children and knew that what she said was true. He signaled to the other men, and they came over to him to confer.

"Moving down the trail to is going to be slow," Declinn said. "Lieutenant Bonny did a hell of sight better than we could have hoped for but now its up to us; I think we gotta hold the Hurons here and let the women folk go ahead." The other three men agreed but the shortest of them, Caleb raised one objection.

"I think one of us had better take point with the group, it'll be easy to lose that trail in some of those patches, 'specially when it gets full dark with the moon startin' to shrink."

"How we gonna choose up?" Micah, the third man asked.

"Straws?" Jason, the last man asked.

"Ain't much choice, for one of us," Declinn said to the other man, "You got a wife at home expecting, Micah."

"'Bout how I see it too," Caleb agreed.

"Works for me," Jason agreed.

Micah, who was a few years younger than the other three, looked like he wanted to object but he saw the other men were set in their decision, so he just nodded. "You'll need my rifle, I 'spect." He handed his weapon, powder horn and shot pouch to the tall sculptor.

"Thanks," Declinn said. "Best be getting a move on as soon as they can stand to start walking."

The four men moved among the survivors encouraging them and seeing to minor wounds so that in less than thirty minutes they were all ablet to get to their feet.

"You're staying behind, aren't you," Declinn's sister asked when he came to stand beside her. The two had talked at their rests on the trail and she had told him all she had seen with the Indian shaman at the massacre. They both knew how important it was to stop the Huron leader.

"It seems the thing to do," he said matter-of-factly. He kept his eyes back up the trail the way they had come, as if afraid to look into his sibling's eyes.

"I don't want to lose you too, big brother," she said. Their family resemblance was starkly visible in their eyes, intense, grey flecks of flint with an inner fire. She reached up to pat him on the cheek with a pointing finger in an old gesture of affection from their childhood.

"I'm too big to lose, sis, you know that. You just concentrate on getting back to the Kingsborough; I promise I'll be along presently."

'No," she said. "I can shoot almost as well as you; we can both cover the retreat of the others." The siblings locked eyes, and the tall sculptor knew better than to argue with her. He shrugged and shook his head.

"Da always said Ma was an unstoppable force," Declinn said, "And you took after her more than him." It was settled then. Deirdre made her goodbyes to the other women.

There was much hugging and some sobs, but the women and children moved off with renewed energy toward the deer path through the mountains on the way back to the fort at Kingsborough in silence.

The four warriors who remained watched the others until they were out of sight then looked at each other and then set about to delay the inevitable as long as possible knowing they had no chance at all…

CHAPTER EIGHT

THE DEVIL CONFRONTED

The four who stayed behind dragged several fallen trees into a triangle on a slight rise that would allow them to cover all approaches to the trail. They found some shovels and spades with which they built up an earthworks around their improvised fort as well as a short trench leading from it into a copes of trees.

"Just in case we get a chance to sneak away if this all doesn't work out." Declinn said, though none of the other three really thought they would have a chance to use any 'escape' path. And they were ready to make that choice.

The next thing Caleb, Jason, Declinn and Deirdre did was use brush to do their best to cover up the exact path that the survivors had taken in case the Huron got beyond them, though they knew it would only delay pursuit by a short time.

The tracking abilities of the Hurons meant they would find any hidden trail almost immediately and there was really only two destinations the prisoners could go, toward Fort Orn or back toward Kingsborough. Yet every minute purchased was precious so the four took up positions behind their improvised barrier where they could cover the woods path from the lake in a triangulating fire.

There, in silence, they waited.

The smell of death still hung over the settlement, a sickly-sweet smell of burnt flesh that clung to the earth in a low, crawling cloud of smoke.

"A shame we can't bury those folk," Caleb said after a bit. "Seems they deserve a proper send off."

"They are resting with the lord," Deirdre said with quiet conviction. "He has open arms for all the innocent."

"No one ever called me that, Ma'am," Caleb said softly.

This made Deirdre smile, a ghost of her brother's own wry expression. "And the virtuous, brother Caleb," she said. "Rest assured your place by The Lord is waiting."

"If the Wyandot have their way, He may not have to long to wait," Jason said with practical, frontier humor. It made all four of them smile.

+++

Karkuk lead his warriors at a steady but punishing pace, delighting in the energy of his new-young body, staying ahead of his braves most of the time, but also dropping back to cajole a slow runner and encourage all to move faster. In contrast to the usual silent running of most tribes, the shaman led a constant chant with his warriors as a way to continue to build their fanatic belief in his power and their unstoppable cause.

+++

"You know that Mama always worried you would be led down the wrong road by some woman," Deirdre Collins said to her brother.

Declinn gave a small snort of humor. "Only woman in my life, besides you, is my Muse, sis." He kept his eyes ahead on the trail from the lake, knowing that the Huron could appear any moment.

"I guess I'm *that* woman, then," Deirdre whispered softly. "I'm sorry it had to come to this."

"That is no way to talk, sis. We're not doing so badly. Where's your faith?"

The woman sobbed and dropped her head to rest in on her arms in front of her. "I feel so ashamed, Dec, but after I saw what happened to Jacob, I put it all in the back of my mind. I knew I had to be strong for the others and the children, but—but now." She started to cry full out, her shoulders moving as she gulped air. "I just don't understand how Our Heavenly Father could let such evil prosper… my poor Jacob and the others did not deserve to die, especially in the horrible way they did. He was a good and holy man! I just can't go on without him."

"Sis, I don't pretend to understand the ways of The Lord, but you know Jacob would want you to go on. He was a deacon because he believed in more than just this flesh we are—believed all the way. And there is such beauty in the world—the dawn over the hills, a hummingbird just kissing a flower, the feel of a new chick's fuzz."

"But how can I go on with him not beside me at night…"

"He is there, sis, you know that. He hears you, he feels you, he is with you as long as he is in your heart."

"But Dec—"

"I know it will hurt, I know its a rock in your gut with sharp edges, but I swear those sharp edges will dull like stones in a stream over time. You have to hold on to that. You have to do what you would want Jacob to do if he was here and you were not. All we are and all this pain is only passing even the art I make—which I hope will outlast me—will be gone someday. All we can do be here for those we care for and do the best we can while we can."

She took a deep breath and straightened up. "You should have preached beside Jacob, Dec." She sat up straighter and wiped her eyes on her sleeve. "You profess so much to be a rebellious soul, yet you have more faith than me."

"You can't be in these woods and not know that there is more than us,

"We're not doing so bad."

more than just the flesh," he said. "But I also know that nature's way is for every predator there is prey, for every locust there are birds to feed; when there is a fire there is new growth. And now that we have seen the dark evil of Karkuk and his sorcery, I know there is an answer. I know there is a way to defeat him and if it is not us it will be someone, some way. Just have hope."

"Little brother," she said, "Da would be proud of you too."

+++

Just before dusk the Huron chase party came running down the path into the clearing where the main ruins of Willow Creek were with no suspicion that they would have any difficulty. There were twenty of them.

The four whites waited until the group of natives were well clear of the tree line with no cover around them and then opened fire. The first Indians fell, and the line abruptly halted, stunned by the sudden turn of events. Before the natives could bring their own guns to bear, three of the colonists were able to reload and fire again. In that time Declinn unleashed half a dozen arrows that felled four of the Hurons.

The Hurons that dropped to the ground were not sure at first how many had ambushed them and looked everywhere for their attackers. They quickly realized they were not overwhelmed by numbers and just as quickly realized that if they waited for the coming darkness it would provide them the chance to move up on their attackers.

There were three Huron who had been bringing up the rear and all of them had rifles, so they fired on the four defenders at regular intervals to keep them pinned down and allow their compatriots to crawl back for cover.

Karkuk had not ducked, but stood defyingly upright, exhorting his followers to take cover and return fire. He ignored the barrage of the colonists with singular contempt.

The Huron set up their own counter-barrage, but the four colonists had chosen their position well and were well protected from the gunfire. It seemed a stand-off.

Nine Indians had fallen with the first volley, seven dead and two wounded severely. These men were left lying in the field moaning.

Karkuk strode back to his own men and stood mindless of the telling fire.

"I don't care what mumbo-jumbo this fella says," Caleb declared. "I'm takin' his scalp!" He fired a clean shot that put a musket ball directly into Karkuk's forehead.

The shaman stepped back two steps, then shook his head like a wet dog shedding water, but the only mark on him was a pink spot where the ball had hit. His angular face lit in a wide feral grin, and he laughed a cold laugh.

"Land of Goshen!" Caleb exclaimed.

"Father in heaven, it is true," Deirdre gasped. "He said no weapon of man could harm him."

"What are we gonna do?" Jason asked.

"Keep at'em," Declinn said with cold determination. "His braves ain't bullet proof; we can at least take them."

Jason, Caleb, Declinn and Deirdre kept up a rotating fire that did not allow the Hurons to even raise their heads to return much fire. It stayed a solid stand-off with the Hurons making no progress while their seeming impervious leader stood above them and exhorted them to keep the whites from escaping.

The shadows lengthened as the day moved toward the purple of twilight. Both sides knew that the state of things could not stay as they were for long; darkness would allow the Hurons to slip out of the gun sights of the defenders. It would be an easy thing then for the Indians to overwhelm the whites.

"I think you outght'a slip off now, sis," Delinn whispered after a time. "They are gonna make a run at us for sure in the next hour or so and I don't have any illusion that we can hold them off; we've done our job delaying them as long as possible. We can buy a few more minutes if you—."

"You know you're the runner the family, Dec," she said with a determined smile that mirrored his own often worn expression. "I wouldn't make it a mile before they caught me."

"Just like ma; stubborn to a fault."

"Nicest thing you've ever said to me, Dec."

"Love you too, sis."

Karkuk obviously became impatient with waiting with his warriors, so he stepped from among his braves and arrogantly stood ahead of them again.

"You will not stop us, Englishmen," the warrior shaman called in English. "You are foolish to resist the power of Nadie. Surrender now and your deaths will quick—if not I will make you suffer as none ever before you."

"Oh, shut up, ya big windbag!" Jason shouted. He fired shot at the Indian and his bullet slammed directly into the center of Karkuk's chest.

The shaman staggered back and dropped to his knees which caused his followers to gasp with shock but almost immediately he jumped straight upright with a deep, mad sounding laugh.

Even in the fading light the spot where the ball had stuck Karkuk chest was clearly unblemished. The musket ball had not even scratched the shaman. The Huron sent up a cheer that became sinister laughter.

"I figured why not try again!" Jason said with a shake of his head. "Shouldn't have wasted a ball on the devil!"

A second roar of triumph went up from the Huron warriors as their leader and they popped to their feet ready to press the attack.

"He said no weapon of man could harm him," Deirdre said in a hushed tone. "He was not lying."

The four colonists charged their guns to prepare, but then Declinn abruptly stopped in mid action and set his rifle down.

"I think I have it, sis." Declinn nodded his head as if in answer to a question he had asked himself. "Yes, that is it, the answer." Before she could ask what he meant, he stood up.

"Karkuk," Declinn yelled in a voice strong enough to cut through the cheers of the braves, "I declare you are a coward! You have power, but no heart; you would let his followers die while you are standing unhurt. I declare you are a false shaman!"

The Huron warriors stopped cheering and after they realized what the woodsman had said. They started to surge forward but Karkuk held up his hands to stop them.

"Declinn," Deirdre whispered, "What are you doing?"

"What I can," he said. "I have an idea but just be ready to shoot like blazes if I mess this up."

"I know you, the one they call Tall Oak—the Image Maker," The shaman called back. "The Gods speak to you as well. but your white ears cannot hear the true Gods of this forest clearly."

The sculptor boldly stepped forward in front of their makeshift log fort, fully exposing himself to any impulsive Huron's gunfire, but none shot at him, so amazed were they by his audacious actions.

"I hear clearly enough," Declinn said in the Wyandot language. "I hear the trees speak to me to make my art. And now I hear a dog barking, one who hides behind trickery and lies."

The frontiersman strode forward, arms outstretched, leaving his powder horn and shot pouch behind but with his pack still slung over his shoulder. He walked directly toward the Huron leader, passing the dead and wounded braves. He passed between several of the most advanced of the Indian warriors as if they did not matter.

When he came to within ten feet of Karkuk himself, Declinn halted. They were of a height with broad chests and wide shoulders, Declinn with his long black hair and the Indian with his shaven head and single scalp lock.

Both men exuded a calm certainty that set them apart from all who stood around them, so much so that the Huron warriors actually stepped back from the pair in anticipation of what might come. The two men were eye to eye, almost mirror images of each other, like titans of old preparing for a cosmic event.

"You are blind to the true powers I possess," Karkuk's voice was a low rumble from somewhere beyond time and space. His tone was not boasting now, speaking matter-of-factly and almost with a sadness for the ignorance of the man before him, like an adult speaking to a child who just did not understand.

"I saw you shake off musket balls," Declinn said, "but your braves are not bullet proof. You are protected by your God, but they are just toys for you to throw before the English guns. Do they mean so little to you to be slaughtered for your Nadie's pleasure?" He spoke loud enough for all the braves to hear him and noticed that they were listening intently.

The Indian leader's eyes flashed with anger, and he raised his hands above his head in a gesture of summoning. "They will now see that I will lead our people from the darkness of the white invaders into the light of a new age. You will feel the power of the Nadie and see how I will stop all English and French guns!" He moved his fingers, and the sculptor felt a strange surge of energy through his whole form that caused him to stagger back.

"Declinn!" Deirdre gasped, almost rising to her feet at what she saw. She began to pray silently, her knuckles white as she kept her rifle aimed at the nearest Indian to her brother.

In the gathering dark, a ghostly glow of power was clearly visible as it pulsed from and gathered about the muscular form of Karkuk. It was like a flickering candlelight that illuminated the area all around him, casting an orange yellow glow across Declinn's features.

The sculptor reacted to the sensations that the sorcerer was calling down on him by throwing a punch that connected with the Huron. He threw the blow from his feet, twisting his whole body and the full force of his two hundred and thirty pounds and all his accumulated hatred for the shaman and what he had done.

The force of the blow and its unexpected nature staggered the Indian who took two steps back. There was a collective gasp from the stunned watching braves.

Declinn then launched himself forward to slam into the sorcerer so that both men went to the ground. They rolled over with the sculptor getting his powerful hands around the throat of the Huron.

Some of Karkuk's men made to move toward the struggling giants but others restrained them, enjoying the conflict and certain that it would be another demonstration of their red Messiah's ultimate power.

Karkuk himself seemed less certain. His eyes bugged out as the steel corded fingers of the frontiersman tightened around his windpipe. The copper skinned shaman stared into the fierce grey eyes of the man above him and saw a savagery and force of will what was equal to his own.

Karkuk smashed an elbow into Declinn's side at the same time he shifted his weight and toppled the sculptor off of him. Both men rose to their feet like cats and separated. That was when Declinn drew a hatchet and went into a fighting crouch.

The shaman features lit with real humor, and he tilted his head back offering his open throat to the weapon. And he laughed again. Karkuk's laugh was full-bodied, and his warriors joined him in bellows of mirth.

"I can not be hurt by your weapons, Image Maker." The Huron leader proclaimed. "I will enjoy most specially watching the light of the Great Spirit's life leaving your body."

He stepped in close to the look straight into the sculptor's eyes in the last fading rays of the dying sun. He gestured with subtle intent and agony twitched through the limbs of the sculptor.

Declinn grit his teeth and fought to move his right hand and arm as the gestured energy of the shaman worked to overpower him.

"When I have crushed you, I will do the same to all the English and then the French in our land. Soon the forest gods will speak clearly again, and they will sing the song of The People and name me champion."

The sorcerer looked hard into the struggling white man's eyes, enjoying the struggle he could sense there, the expression of agony crept across Declinn's face.

Deirdre sobbed in horror as she watched her brother's body twitch and writhe in agony her mind recalling what had been done to her husband. Once more the horrific transformation she had witnessed flashed before her eyes. Her fingers tightened on her long rifle and she prepared to raise it, not to fire at the shaman, but to put her brother out of his misery so the same transformation would not happen to Declinn.

The hatchet dropped from the Declinn's palsied fingers as he snarled defiance at the sorcerer. "If I go to hell, Karkuk, I'm sure as the devil is taking you with me."

"Fool," the shaman said, "No weapon of any man can harm me."

Declinn yelled a curse and snaked his hand into the side-pack he still wore. When he pulled his hand free, he held a familiar object in his clenched fist.

The sculptor thrust the object forward with all the strength and hate he could muster. The razor-sharp edge sliced through the neck muscles of the Indian to lodge into the bones of his throat with a fount of blood.

The Huron leader staggered back from the mesmerized sculptor, his lips moving as he tried to form words. "How?"

"My wood chisel is not a weapon," Declinn said flatly. "It's a tool of my trade."

The shaman could not hear him by this time. Instead, the Huron holy man's eyes went wide, his mouth moved without sound then he gave a convulsive shudder and toppled over dead.

When Karkuk's body hit the ground, he was no longer the powerful giant who had led the rebellion. Now his form was now the shriveled old body of the old man that he had been. Immediately the form of the shaman began to decay, all the energy that had filled it to give it the image of youthful vigor flowing off it like heat waves on a hot rock surface. His form shrunk, his flesh decayed and Karkuk, vessel of Nadie, savior of his people was no more.

EPILOGUE

THE DETAILS OF THE DEVIL

The Huron warriors were so stunned by the sudden loss of their leader that they could not even feel anger or fury in the immediate confusion. They stood staring at the fallen leader trying to absorb the enormity of the sudden turnaround.

Jason, Caleb and Deirdre took advantage of the confusion to fire at the exposed braves, killing two of them immediately then snatched up their second rifles to fire again.

The spell was broken then, and the other Huron charged the four colonials with vengeful cries of anger.

Two of the braves launched themselves at Declinn.

The first Huron swung a war club at the sculptor's head, but the frontiersman ducked the wild swing driving a shoulder hard into the Indian's sternum. There was cracking sound, and the Indian warrior was bowled over.

The second brave had a knife and a slash from it caught the sculptor across the upper arm and back. Declinn was about to whirl to face him when there was a volley of rifle fire that slammed into the running native.

"Run you bloody devils!" the voice of Grover cut through the gunpowder smoke followed by the yells from the other riflemen from Fort Orn.

The Hurons that were not shot in the first volley turned and fled into the darkness of the woods.

"I got to the fort while the Hurons were staked out around it waiting to spring their trap," the woodsman said as he and Caleb embraced. "I snuck around them and warned the troops from Kingsborough; we ambushed the ambushers. Wiped'em all out, by golly."

"Oh Declinn!" Deirdre threw her arms around her brother, and he wrapped his good arm around her shoulders.

"This the big chief that caused it all?" The late arrival said as he stood over the frail looking corpse of Karkuk. "He don't look like much to me."

Declinn knelt down and removed his bloody chisel from the dead shaman's throat. "Oh, he was," the sculptor said as he cleaned off the tool on his buckskin breeches, "but he forgot that when you make a deal with a devil you have to read the fine print: it's the details that matter."

THE HOUND OF O'ROURKE

CHAPTER ONE

A PATH OF DESTRUCTION?

Tommy Mahoney walked beside the O'Rourke Family wagon as it clattered along the forest road. He kept stumbling because he seldom looked down at the trail as his eyes were mostly on redhaired Mary O'Rourke. Mary sat beside her gruff driver-servant Shamus O'Toole and shyly pretended to ignore the gangly Tommy's glances.

Each time the boy stumbled head-long, often falling on his face, the colleen could not help from acknowledging him with a chuckle. It was a very un-lady-like half-snort and half burp.

When Tommy fell, he felt the color rise in his face, but he pushed himself to his feet. He brushed himself off in an attempt to approximate a look of dignity. And each time he recovered he was a miserable failure at it. After all, it was hard to look very dignified when one's breeches were patched, one's shirt was threadbare, and both were thick with fresh grime.

It is not that he was an unhandsome lad, if somewhat underfed. He had a pleasant, homely face, sandy hair and wide staring blue eyes that, in a higher class of fellow, might have been called 'poets' eyes. But there-in lie poor Tommy's problem, he was a bondsman, and the lovely Mary O'Rourke was the daughter of landed gentry from County Cork. She and her folk had come to make their mark on the new world of North America. And that placed her far above his pitiful station.

Even if she had not been the beautiful redhaired daughter of his master Tommy would have thought her far too good for him. She was so self-possessed and pretty, her green eyes sparkling with humor and wit, her full lips like slices of peaches. And when she spoke her voice was music to the tall youth sweeter than the song of any bird.

Still, ever since she had come to her father's estate in Virginia, Tommy had dreamed at night of walking beside her. He just had not thought that walking it would be down a forest trail on the way to the far-off Fort Pitt.

"Master Mahoney," Mary said coyly, "Is the path so rugged that you can not keep your feet upon it?" Her words had humor beneath them, but Tommy did not feel that she was making fun of him. He felt as if she were singing to him by just saying his name.

"Just a few stray roots, Mistress O'Rourke," he stammered, "But I am grateful for your concern."

"Enough of that, boy," the burly wagon driver called down. "We're coming up to the German's Inn so run ahead and let them know we will require a good room for the lady and quarters for the rest of us."

"Aye, Master O'Toole, that I shall," The boy said. He cast a last glance up at the giggling girl and then scampered off ahead of the slow-moving convoy of five wagons.

"You have the bit o' the devil in you, girl." O'Toole said when Tommy was gone. "You will give that boy a heart attack acting that way, Mistress Mary, of that I am most certain."

She laughed out loud. "I certainly hope not, Shamus, else who will entertain me once we reach the fort? He is all that has made this constant jostling upon these forest roads bearable."

+++

Declinn Blayde was far ahead of the O'Rourke wagon train, and he was very worried.

The darkhaired, woodsman was crouched by the side of the trail with his Philadelphia Long Rifle cradled across his thighs while studied the woods on either side. The trail to Fort Pitt wound through a number of hills along a path that paralleled a nameless creek. The trail was beneath a bluff that overlooked the roughhewn path creating a stretch of road that was almost a green canyon.

Standing, Declinn would have been a tall man with long jet-black hair that hung wild over his broad, muscular shoulders. His clothes were a homespun shirt, buckskin trousers and jacket and high moccasins with Delaware beading on them.

He had been crouched in the foliage for almost a quarter hour after working his way silently through the woods off the road because of an odd feeling.

His flint grey eyes scanned the whole of the area with the experience of one who had grown up in the wilderness. He was well aware that his life, and those he was guiding, depended on his keen senses.

Now those senses told him that something was not right at all.

He could not tell exactly what. There were no obvious tracks on the trail and no tell-tale signs in the woods. There *were* clear marks of the last train that passed along the path but from all indications that had been two days before. There were clear animal signs, deer spoor and the tracks of a small cougar that was hunting those deer, but no traces of human passage since the last wagon train.

The birds still sang in the trees and the small beasts of the woods seemed to be going about their daily routines of foraging with no break that indicated anything to be alarmed by. Yet still, some inner sense told him something was wrong. The skin on the back of his neck prickled as if he were in a stiff breeze. That always meant trouble.

Declinn had learned to trust his instincts, so now he squatted unmoving in the thick undergrowth, becoming part of the forest itself to try and feel what exactly was amiss. And he quietly watched.

The frontiersman had been engaged as a scout for the O'Rourke party on the journey through to Fort Pitt and had been moving ahead of the party of five wagons when he became aware of his odd feeling.

Now he crouched unmoving and looked ahead trying to see with his inner eye what was making his inner senses tingle.

Ain't nothing I can see or hear, he thought. *So why am I sure things are catawampus?* Then, he finally realized what had triggered the feeling.

That smell! The wind was blowing away from him but for a moment an errant gust blew on an angle that brought the scent to him that he sniffed. It was a sweet smell that was not the natural scent of flowers; it was man made— a cologne or hair pomade of some sort. He must have smelled a trace of it before for the briefest of moments and unconsciously it had triggered his sense of danger.

Ain't no reason there should be a perfumed person out there in the woods, the frontiersman thought. *Least ways not any good reason*. He rechecked the ground to be sure that his first impressions of the trail were correct, that the last human passage was days hence.

No doubt the last folks through here were those two wagons at least two days ago. He wanted to stretch his long legs but stayed as he, as still as a part of the landscape. He was looking at the treetops to gauge the wind direction and trying to think which way it was blowing when he smelled that too human scent.

He set about staring harder at the foliage across the road now, knowing if he was still enough, if he truly became part of the landscape, let his human mind fade so that he became one with nature, he would see something at some point and hopefully they—if there was someone—they would not see him.

Before he could discover anything, the wind brought something else, a sound from down the trail. It was the last thing he would have ever expected to hear in the woods, though it would not have been so odd in a different location, like a tavern late at night— it was someone singing a song of the late war, very off key.

Come all ye young men all, let this delight you,
Cheer up ye, young men all, let nothing fright you,
Never let your courage fail when you're brought to trial,
Nor let your fancy move at the first denial.

So then this gallant youth did cross the ocean,
To free America from her invasion,
He landed at Quebec with all his party,
The city to attack, being brave and hearty.

It was a high-pitched male voice, and the woodsman could not help but crack a slight smile. He recognized the warbling as belonging to the young bondsmen from the O'Rourke party, Tommy Mahoney.

Didn't reckon that the wagons could have caught up with me yet, Blayde thought, *but its not a good thing if there is trouble come on. I better find out what it is and fast!*

+++

Bear Collins was a man whose stature and demeanor fit his name. He wore an old bearskin robe that made his massive form look even bigger than it was. His thick matted red beard and long red hair was combed back with great care to cover a balding spot. The hair was slicked down with great care with pomade he had stolen from a trading post on the Ohio. The hair pomade was his only vanity. His fingernails were dirty, his patched breeches were greasy and his rawhide moccasins thin with wear.

Collins had wedged his great bulk in between a split in a granite rock that overlooked a section of the trail in front of the rise he was on. Below him, in the dense brush that bordered the trail, he had ten Huron confederates waiting for the trader's wagon train. A scout down trail had spotted the rich prize three days before and run up trail to alert Collins and his gang.

Bear had chosen this stretch of road to ambush the wagons because with the river across the road beyond the ridge and the rough hills where he was concealed, the people in the wagons would have nowhere to go when the attack occurred.

He suspected that the little caravan was a rich prize and looked forward to the debauchery that the spoils would buy him, particularly a Huron squaw he had a mind to purchase from her father.

If the prize was all he hoped, he might even buy some land and be able to pass himself off as 'respectable' to some frontier settlement. Bear was tired of the hit and run life, which while it had kept him fed for years, would be too dangerous now that the war between France and England was done. Law and order might find its way to the woods and that would not be good for men like Bear.

The highwayman was roused from his thoughts of booty by a strange sound coming from up the trail and it took him a moment to realize it was someone singing. Badly.

"*The French drew up their men, for death prepared.*

In one another's face the armies stared,
While Wolfe and Montcalm together walked,
Between their armies they like brothers talked."

Collins signaled with a birdcall to the braves below and the others up the trail. It seemed odd that he had not heard the wagons but then he saw the single figure round the corner of the road, a gangly blond-haired boy.

+++

Tommy Mahoney sang with joy as he strode swiftly down the twisting trail toward the inn, moving at a good pace. He was smiling so wide he thought his face would crack. Mary O'Rourke had actually spoken to him and with concern for his well-being before sending him on his journey as herald for the wagon train.

"*Each man then took his past at their retire.*
So, then these numerous hosts began to fire,
The cannon on each side did roar like thunder,
And youths in all their pride were torn asunder.

And it is a short journey from good Christian concern to romantic delight, he thought. As he sang the next verse he happened to look directly across the trail to his left and saw a bright red spot in the green.

"*The drums did loudly beat, colors were flying,*
The purple gore did stream and men lay dying,
When shot off from his horse fell this brave hero,
And we lament his loss in weeds of sorrow."

He faltered in his singing for a moment; his eye caught sight of something red in the foliage across the road from him. *I wonder what that is?* He thought just as the brave beneath the red feather rose from the bush to draw a bead on Tommy's head with a nocked arrow on his bow.

CHAPTER TWO

SPIRIT OF THE WOODS

Tommy froze in his tracks with his mouth agape. His body began to shake as he saw the native rise with death in his eyes.

As the Huron pulled the string back to full draw there was a sudden explosion from the woods high up to Tommy's right. As the boy watched the Indian warrior did a back flip that looked like a marionette that had been thrown away by a child.

“Run boy, run!” Declinn Blayde called from behind the cloud of smoke from his long rifle as he set to reloading.

Tommy’s legs seemed to move of their own accord as almost a dozen more feathered heads rose from the bushes across from him and came charging toward him.

Branches slapped the toe-headed boy when he dove into the woods but then he suddenly found himself beside the mountainous Declinn Blayde while the frontiersman calmly finished reloaded his long rifle.

The long gun roared, this time again right past Tommy’s ear defining him. The boy was paralyzed by the shot until the tall scout grabbed the boy’s shoulder and shoved him.

“Go boy, run back to the train and warn the others!”

Tommy got ‘on top’ of his legs then and, with only a side glance at the wall of Indians that were charging across the road at the two whites, he redoubled his speed.

The boy ran down toward the creek while behind him Blayde smashed the first of the attackers with the butt of his rifle. After the brave fell, the frontiersman was forced to turn and race to catch up with Tommy.

“Keep moving boy,” Blayde called as he loaded his rifle with practiced ease as he sprinted up beside Tommy. “Cut through the woods. If the sound of this little tussle doesn’t warn the wagon train, then you’ll have to do it yourself.”

Arrows from the attacking natives whizzed all around the two running colonists, sounding like a swarm of angry wasps. The shafts added wings to young Mahoney’s feet, and he redoubled his effort. He slid, scurried and stumbled down the embankment to the gurgling stream ignoring the pebbles that made for treacherous footing. He had never moved so fast or stayed so upright for so long before in his short life.

There was another rifle report from Balyde’s gun and a grunt of pain. The running feet behind the two fleeing whites stopped for only a moment.

Declinn strong strides brought him up beside the fleeing lad.

“Up the ridge,” Blayde called in a steady voice. He was not even breathing hard as he kept up with the boy. The two veered into the dense underbrush.

While he ran Blayde was loading powder and shot into his long rifle, finally spitting a lead ball down the barrel then tamping it down with a rod without even breaking stride.

The sound of the pursuers pushing through the dense forest growth came closer, the Huron eschewing their usual silent stalking to whoop in anticipation of taking the two scalps as trophies.

“Keep moving,” Blayde ordered. He suddenly spun and fired behind them again, then resumed running.

Abruptly Declinn and Tommy were at the top of the ridge to come out onto a wide grassy hill.

Tommy's legs gave out then and he sprawled full length on his face, panting heavily, his lungs feeling like they were on fire. "I can't go on," he managed to gasp. "I'm sorry; you keep going."

"You take a little breather, boy," the frontiersman spoke with no rancor in his tone and a ghost of a smile on his lips. "I'll get me a little bit shootin' practice in while we dawdle." He then proceeded to send lead bullets at the attackers as rapidly as he could fire and reload his gun. He moved smoothly, with unhurried, practiced skill so that each discharge of the long gun had deadly results.

The seven attackers that were left in the advancing horde were armed only with bow, arrows and tomahawks. The woodsman's rifle helped equalize the odds with the lightening quick fire from Blayde causing them to dive for cover. Once concealed behind shrubs and rocks they attempted to snipe at their white prey.

Declinn and Tommy found themselves at the top of the steep hill with only the speed of the woodsman's rifle able to keep the Huron from making a concerted rush up the gradient. The slope helped in keeping the fire of their bows from being accurate, shooting up toward the sun.

"The train should hear this ruckus from on top of this hill for sure," Blayde said as he tipped powder into his rifle's pan to fire again. "So, there's no need for you to run to them now, lessin' you want to, Tommy."

"I'm just fine right here, sir," the boy said between gulps of air as he sat up. He picked up a stout tree branch as a cudgel and took a practice swing with it, "I just had me a nice lie down for a bit, don't cha' know."

Despite the circumstance the rugged shooter smiled. "That's the attitude, boy," he said. "I don't think you'll need that though. I think these fellas are about ready to leave us themselves for the noise we've made."

Just at that moment one of the Huron braves, that had slipped up-stream unseen and had worked his way along the ridge, sprang out of cover at Blayde.

The Huron swung a tomahawk at the woodsman's head, but Tommy saw the movement and yelled, "Duck!" in time for Blayde to dodge the first attack. Before the Indian could swing again Tommy had popped up and broke his makeshift wooden club into the brave's face.

Declinn drew his knife and stabbed the Huron in the heart then grabbed up his rifle again. The woodsman fired a shot from the hip at the charging Hurons down the hill as they popped up to take advantage of the sneak attack.

It was an exceptional shot from the frontiersman that killed one of them who had dared to lead the charge. The remarkable shot broke their spirit, and they stopped and dropped to ground once more.

Suddenly a whistle from up the hill summoned the braves and the surviving attackers turned to run back down the hill. In a few moments they had disappeared once again into the forest.

There was an eerie moment of silence following the cacophony of the battle before birds began to sing again and Tommy asked, "Are they really gone?" He stared at the broken club, smeared with blood, then crawled up to beside the rifleman to peer down the ridge to the woods.

"I think so," Blayde said, "but best to keep an eye for a bit, they ain't as sneaky as white men, but they can come real close. Almost as clever as Europeans when it comes to finding new ways to part a fella's hair."

The gangly boy looked up at him without rising from his prone position. "Why do you say that? You sound more like a redskin than a white man."

"I take that as a compliment," Blayde smiled. His flint grey eyes scanned the shadows of the hillside for any more sign of the attackers. "I grew up on the north frontier in the Mohawk Valley where my father was a trapper. We wintered with the Mohican tribe of for a few years. It was a good life and a good education. It was more than enough education, in fact, that I discovered in the summers when we would go to rendezvous or into Albany, that a store-bought suit often was draped over a liar or a cheat." He finished reloading his rifle, wryly demonstrating his powder horn was now empty. If the Hurons returned it would be one shot and then hand-to-hand. "You do know that Indians don't lie, don't you?"

"Come on now," Tommy scoffed. He became brave enough to sit up and look around, relieved to see no movement down in creek bed. "They are the same as anyone. My Da said so, anyway."

"Well," Blayde said standing and stretching like a great cat. "He's right in most respects, and quite progressive for a Virginia man, but they are not exactly the same as white men. Ain't near as obsessed with getting things and keeping things. Nor with lording over things as white folks seem to be. They see the world different they consider life a gift from the Sky People and life has to be lived with honor."

The boy prickled. "We understand honor in Virginia, sir."

"I know you do, son," The woodsman said with a gentle smile. "Or else you would have left me in the thick of things, for which I'm much obliged."

He hoisted his rifle over his shoulder and turned to head across the grassy slope in the direction where the wagon train would be coming from. "But most white men seem to treat honor like it was a Sunday sort of feeling; something to be practiced in church only. To the Huron— what English folk call the Wyandot- and the Mohicans, and all the red men I've ever met, they consider the whole world their church. Means they just don't lie. Oh, it's a generalization I suppose, but I've never met an Indian that lied." He laughed and then added, "Sometimes they might not tell you the *whole* truth unless you ask the right question, but never an outright lie."

The two white men were in the tree line by now and the difference in the

He picked up a stout tree branch…

quality of sound made Tommy lower his voice to a reverential tone. "I guess you would know sir, but what do you think that attack was about? Are these Wyandot on the warpath again?"

"No," Blayde said with certainty. "No paint. No rifles. Seems they were intent on banditry pure and simple; they would have been in bigger numbers if they were on the war trail." His voice took on a sudden strained tone and he leaned against a tree while looking behind them.

"You might best go ahead, Tommy to make sure the train is alright, I'll just rest here a bit."

"What's wrong?" The boy saw that the color was draining from the tall woodsman's face. Then he noticed there was blood on the buckskin of Blayde's jacket.

"By Saint Michael, you're bleeding."

CHAPTER THREE

MASKS OF DEATH

"I caught an arrow somewhere back there while we were running," the Blayde said with a grimace. "It's a bit of an annoyance." He leaned against the tree and began to sway, shaking his head to clear his vision.

"Let me see!" Tommy moved to the frontiersman and could see the shaft of the arrow protruding from the man's left side where he had not seen it before. "My goodness!" The shaft had a growing red stain around it over the lower back of the tall woodsman. His jacket was pinned to his left side.

"Break it off, lad, but leave the tip it in me," Blayde said with a forced smile, "It will keep me plugged like a cork in a bottle till we can get it out properly. Then you get on your way to be sure the train knows what happened."

"No," Tommy said. "I'll break it off for you, but I'm not leaving you on your own, them savages might come back."

The boy braced one hand against the woodsman's side and grabbed the feathered end of the shaft with the other. He did his best to immobilize the man's side then and with considerable effort to not pull on the wound itself, he gave a sharp twist and snapped the shaft off.

Blayde grunted and shivered in pain but made no complaint. "Nicely done, Master Mahoney, and I appreciate the thought, but now you have to get to that train."

"I'm sorry, sir, but it seems to me if them devils' come back you would be in a bad way here alone as you have no more powder for your rifle." He looked around and found a second stout stick and picked it up to show he was ready for battle again.

"Ain't rightly true," Declinn said with a weak grin, "I got one whole shot left; but I appreciate you staying to keep me company; I'm pretty sure the party heard all the ruckus anyway."

Tommy, despite his fear of the returning Hurons, stood up a bit taller, pushing his shoulder's back that the frontiersman had allowed him to remain. The boy was about to ask what was next when his eyes widened noticed a detail on the oak tree that Blayde leaned against. "Look at that!" He pointed to a section of the tree where a large circle had been cut out of the trunk. Down near the base of the tree were the ashes of a recent fire and shavings of bark.

"Some brave thought this tree was good medicine," the woodsman explained. He ran a hand along the surface of the tree, appreciating the texture and shapes of the cutout shape as only a sculptor who worked in wood could. It was what the frontiersman did to support himself most of the time and was renowned for his creations across the colonies.

"What do you mean?" Tommy asked.

"The Iroquois believe that the evil spirits that cause disease could be scared away by special masks." Declinn said with a harsh whisper, his side obviously hurting him more. "They build the masks into a live tree, and the Iroquois would carve a face on the tree resembling a tree spirit or a healing spirit. To make the mask, a brave walks through the woods until he finds a tree whose spirit talks to him. He talks to the tree, builds a fire, sprinkles tobacco, then strips bark from the tree. He outlines a face and cuts out the section to the tree he outlined."

"Seems kind of silly," Tommy said as he peered more closely at the stripped space, "talking to trees and such."

Blayde laughed, "No more so than white folks praying to statues of saints or your folks in Ireland talking to the little people. And I sort of do it to every piece of wood I work on, looking to see whatever soul the wood has for me to bring out in my sculpture."

The boy colored and shrugged. "I guess not when you look at it that way, but it's just a big hole in the tree shaped like, well, like a head." He reached out to touch the empty space where the tree had been cut open. It felt oddly warm to him, and he felt—or imagined he felt— as if a tiny charge of lightning sprang from the trunk to his hand. He jumped back, startled.

"The section of the tree with the face is cut out and an animal tail is sometimes added." Blayde continued his voice faltering a little as he dealt with his pain from the arrow wound. He enjoyed the young man's startled expression. "Then the brave goes into a secluded shelter to carve the mask. He polishes then decorates it with hair, feathers, etc. The men chant, dance, and sing wearing the mask to ward off the evil spirits that caused the sickness. It is a solemn a prayer as them folks can make."

"Still seems a bit silly to me," Tommy said, "but no offense to them that believe." His eyes were beginning to strain as he scanned the trail behind in fear and ahead in hope for the wagon train. In a few moments he saw movement ahead. "Look!"

Coming through the trees were three of the wagoneers with rifles at the ready moving toward them.

"I guess they did hear the ruckus." Blayde said. "I think we can finally take a deep breath, eh? And I suspect you will be quite the game cock when we get back."

"What?" the boy asked as he helped the muscular woodsman to stand and move downhill to greet the new arrivals.

"Well, lad," the exhausted woodsman said, "You are the one who found the ambush; you saved the wagon train, and my hide as well when you brained that brave at the start of it."

"I did?"

"You sure did," Blayde said with a sly smile. "And that's the way I'm gonna tell it."

"Jehoshaphat!" The color drained from the boy's face as it he had been shot with an arrow himself. "I guess I did."

Declinn Blayde laughed. "Let's let those guys know we're here, finish your song, boy."

Tommy laughed with him and piped up.

"The French began to break, their ranks were flying,
Wolfe seemed to revive while he lay dying,
He lifted up his head as his drums did rattle,
And to his army said, How goes the battle?
His aide-de-camp replied, Tis in our favor,
Quebec, with all her pride, nothing can save her,
She falls into our hands with all her treasure,
Oh then, brave Wolfe replied, I die with pleasure."

+++

"How could you miss that big lunk, Blayde?" Bear Collins barked at his Huron allies. "You're supposed to be the best trackers and hunters in the woods." The Indian survivors of the attack were huddled in their camp two miles from the attack site. They were not looking happy at the dressing down that Collins was giving them, their normal stoicism not evident.

"He who is The-image-maker," Machk, the leader of the Huron renegades said using their name for Declinn Blayde, "Is like a ghost in the woods. His medicine is strong."

"Bahh!" Bear said. "He's just the luckiest son of perdition that ever scurried on two legs." He ran a hand along his bearded cheek remembering a slap he had received from Blayde at a tavern two years before. The tall woodsman had caught Collins cheating at cards and when Bear disputed him there had been a fight but, rather than beating Bear cleanly, Blayde had slapped him. Then he made Bear confess to his crime in front of the whole inn.

Collins had wanted to find a way to get even since then; now with Declinn hired to guide the O'Rourke party he not only had that chance but could make a profit on the deal as well.

"Yes," Machk agreed. "Image-maker has luck, much good medicine. He killed three of my warriors." His expression darkened. "You promised much money and guns if we attack wagons, you say they be easy dead. We did the attack, but they were not easy dead."

"And you'll get your money," Collins promised. "And the much rum that I promised." This made the Hurons all grunt with annoyance. They had heard that promise before, now too many times.

"You say we get before, but we not get," one of the Indians spat.

"You will get it, I swear it," Bear studied the faces of the braves and went into his full salesman voice. "The O'Rourke train is carrying a fortune for that avaricious nobleman to set up a business at Fort Pitt—money in Continental currency and jewels, but more important, his personal treasure, his daughter. That's why I told you no guns; you are better shots with those bows. If we get her, there is nothing O'Rourke will not do, nothing we can't have for the asking. More money than we've ever seen before."

"You told us, no kill woman." Machk insisted. "But they not come, only Tall Oak."

"We'll get them at the German's Inn," Bear said. "I promise it will be worth it; he'll give us a king's ransom for the girl, you'll get all the guns and rum you can ever want. And I'll rub that self-righteous Blayde's face in his own failure!"

CHAPTER FOUR

TRUNK TROUBLES

Back at the O'Rourke Wagon Train, Tommy was indeed feted as a hero just as Blayde had predicted. The scouts from the train were able to get the wounded woodsman back on an improvised litter and the arrow was removed, the wound cleaned then tightly bound with no difficultly. There was no more trouble along the trail with everyman of the train eagle-eyed with their rifles loaded and scanning the path.

"But I just don't understand, why wouldn't the redskins use guns?" The driver Shamus asked Blayde, who had been convinced to ride with him for the remainder of the journey. It was not long before they reached the compound of Erich Von Stuben's Tavern and Inn on the high road to Fort Pitt. "That seems a bit too unlikely they wouldn't have guns if they were planning some sort of mischief; the Wyandot have had guns for a long time."

"I think it is clear that somebody organized them for that attack," Blayde surmised. He was obviously annoyed to be seated beside the wagonmaster, but his employer had insisted. In reality the wound did ache so he was glad for the rest.

The full wagon train moved into the main yard of the Inn complex and began to unhitch the horses. "I think they made a deliberate choice to keep guns out of the braves hands so the column was overtaken before you could fire a shot and alert the Inn. It's why they were all on one side of the train— to just rain arrows on you all without hurting their own men."

"But Indian's just don't fight that way." Shamus said. "They usually just swarm and devil take the hind most!"

"Aye," Declinn agreed. "They don't; it has the earmarks of a devious white man's hand in the planning." He and Shamus exchanged a knowing look but the two of them left it there as the wagon rolled to a stop in the Inn's yard.

The Inn was not a fort, but did have a low split rail and earth works outer wall that framed the five buildings and corrals of the complex. The land directly around it was cleared to give a good field of fire should the need for defense arise—no one living in the wilderness ever really dropped their guard completely.

Blayde looked over at the other wagons and smiled at the sight; Tommy Mahoney was surrounded by several of the other bondsmen who were peppering him with questions about his adventures and near-death experience.

With each retelling the boy's valor grew until he related how he challenged the Wyandot brave he'd kayoed to single combat before defeating him. The part that the darkhaired woodsman had played in the battle seemed to shrink also with each new version of the now epic tale.

Tommy could not lose the grin as he and his fellows unloaded the necessaries for the stay at the Inn— they had planned a three-day stop to service the wagons even before the attack. Now word would be sent ahead so that they might get an escort to meet them from Fort Pitt part way along the road.

All the peer adulation paled for the gangly youth however before the not-so-veiled glances of Mary O'Rourke. The young girl, to the distraction of her chaperone maid, rested on a bench in the courtyard and watched the servants unloading with her eyes fixed on the valiant Mahoney.

"It is unseemly for a young lady to linger so," Maeve, Mary's maid said. She was a sour faced woman with silver hair many said was obtained by over-worrying. She constantly wrung her hands together and made 'tsk-tsk' noises. "People will start to talk, young lady."

"Oh, hush, Maeve, I can sit here in full view to take the air and all propriety is observed. No one can take offense with my actions—or lack of them."

"Propriety, perhaps," the older woman said, "but it does not stop talk at you eying that long legged boy. The go-sips in the tavern will be all a chatter about your—your just encouraging scandalous talk by staring at him!" She seemed flushed at having scolded the teenager and fanned herself with a handkerchief.

"Let them drink ale till they burst and chat till their teeth are worn down," Mary giggled. She waved to Tommy as he pulled an ornate trunk off the back of one of the wagons.

The boy looked up from his labors and saw the girl wave. For a second he thought he might faint with her acknowledgment and lost focus. That moment of distraction caused the wooden case to drop on his right foot.

"God's garters!" he cursed then did a comical jig hopping on the uninjured foot.

"The hero of the Wyandot ambush can't handle a simple box!" one of the other boys taunted.

"Be off with you," Maeve called across the courtyard, shooing the boys with the piercing tone of her voice. "That's not just a box- it's a *trousseau* trunk that has been in Miss O'Rourke's family for five generations; carved it was from a single oak in County Cork."

Indeed, the trunk was intricately carved with scenes from Irish mythology and bound with heavy brass clasps. It had not only an air of age about it but of specialness—and perhaps to Tommy, who had recovered enough to stare at his 'attacker'- of otherworldliness.

"I'm sorry I dropped it, ma'am," Tommy apologized. "I'll take it into Miss Mary's room myself."

"Don't hurt yourself further, Master Thomas," Mary said with a grin. "Else you will not be able to protect me if the red devils return."

Tommy drew himself up to his full height and puffed out his chest. "I could never be so hurt I could not to protect you, Miss O'Rourke." He spoke with such great seriousness that Maeve burst out laughing but Mary did her best to stifle her own giggles.

"I am sure you will," the young girl said with as serious a voice as she could muster. "I am sure you will, Master Mahoney."

Tommy's cheeks colored but he set about wrestling the trunk into the ground floor room that had been chosen for the two women to occupy. Tommy ignored the stares and jeers of the other bondsmen who suddenly found 'other' work to do to avoid helping him. He got the *trousseau* most of the way to the building by dragging it before Declinn Blayde suddenly appeared at his elbow.

"Let me give you a hand there, lad," the frontiersman said. Without waiting for permission, the muscular scout gripped one of the leather straps at the end of the trunk and together the two moved it more easily inside. They placed it in a corner of the girl's room with little more effort.

The tall woodsman ran a practiced hand over the ornate wood carving on the trunk. "This is some of the most beautiful work I've ever seen. The craftsmen who carved this were not just artists; the quality of work is almost magical in the details—the life they gave to the images."

"Miss O'Rourkes nanny mentioned it was really old," Tommy said. "In her family from the old country itself."

"Certainly, old for sure. The craftsman who did has my full admiration; I can only hope create one thing in a lifetime so lifelike."

"What do you mean?"

"Didn't you know, lad," the woodsman said. "When I'm not scouting, I do a bit of carving myself. I just sent off an altar piece I did for a University at Boston last month."

"Golly, I guess lots of things ain't what they seem out here on the frontier, Master Blayde."

"A wise thing to say anywhere, Master Mahoney, always good to look beyond the surface of anything to the real meaning of the thing."

"How's your side?" Tommy did his best to keep up with the seeming inexhaustible woodsman. The boy leaned against the trunk exhausted, his foot was throbbing where the edge of the box had landed.

"Good enough," the scout grinned. "That couple of hours sitting on the wagon did me pretty good. After I can get a full day's rest here, I'll be a healthy as a judge before I head on at dawn."

"A day's rest?" the boy asked. "We shall be here for at least three, Master Shamus said."

"I'd better head out before first light tomorrow and see that all is right up ahead. I might not have you to find the next ambush for me."

Mahoney laughed. "I didn't mean to take all the credit, I mean, the talk sort of make it seem like..."

"Easy, lad," Blayde said. "Enjoy your fame while you can —you did a good deed and truly saved my hide so even if the story that got out ain't exactly chapter and verse the way it happened it's close enough. You and me did what we did together, which makes us comrades-in-arms." He tussled the gangly youth's hair and strode off to the stable to find a meal and a comfortable spot to nest through the rest of the day and evening.

Tommy leaned against the trunk after Declinn had left and, with no one to see his condition, slumped with exhaustion that was deeper than physical. He closed his eyes and tried to rest but all he could see was that arrow in the bow pointed at him and the one sticking out of Declinn's side. And the face of the Wyandot warrior he had hit with the cudgel.

Tommy shivered with returning fear.

Suddenly he felt overwhelmed.

He felt a coward and worse, a fool in front of Mary O'Rourke; no amount of exaggeration of his prowess would hide his clumsiness from her and eventually, as is always the case, the truth would out. Against his will his shoulders began to heave, and tears came salty down his cheeks

"Now, now, me laddie," a brogue voice he had never heard before abruptly made Tommy open his eyes. "Don't be slobberin' all over the trunk, now."

Tommy whirled to see a strangely dressed man standing on the other side of the trunk. He was in the shadows near the back corner of the room, out of the direct light of the window. He was not tall and was slight of build with a thin sliver of a red beard along his thin, narrow chin, but no mustachios. His nose was long and thin as well and slightly hooked over his wide smiling mouth.

"Who are you?" Tommy asked.

"Nin Mac Cuill," the little man said. He stepped into the light from the window and his dark green clothing startled Mahoney as much as the man's sudden appearance; they were of a style of dress half a century old.

"What are you doing in Miss O'Rourke's room, Master Mac Cuill?"

"I come with the trunk, lad," the stranger said as he reached forward and dusted off the top of the trunk with a bright green scarf. "I'm charged to see it, and those that belong with it, safe and sound."

He reached forward and ran a delicate hand over the aged wood and intricate caving of the trunk then his face lit with a broad smile. "This was the tallest oak in the center of a sacred grove in the center of the county in Eire," the little man said. His green eyes glowed as he caressed the carvings of a rampant stag on the trunk lid. "Once the druids danced about it and called on the power of the stars and earth, then the Roman types came and with no regard cut down the holey wood to make such things." There was a great sadness in his voice. "The O'Rourke family were once great warriors who kept to the old ways. Now merchants they be, but still fierce and fearless." He smiled with pride. "And that Mary, she's the fiercest of them all and she has a touch of the 'sight'. Deserves herself a Cuchulainn she does."

"I don't recall seeing you on the wagon train," Tommy looked around the room trying to figure where the little man had come from, wondering why he and Blayde had not seen the fellow when they came in the room. It felt strange and more so for the stories he was telling. "How is that?"

"Oh, I've been around, lad. And I've seen you and your uplifted eyes."

"What do you mean?"

"Oh, boyo," Mac Cuill said. "A blind Britain could see the mongrel eyes you keep focused on the O'Rourke's darlin' damsel."

Tommy bristled at the man's statement and moved to stand by to tower over the smaller man. When he did, the boy noticed that the tips of the man's ears peaked out from the tangle of red hair on the man's head and were slightly pointed.

"You can't talk that way 'bout Miss O'Rourke," the boy said puffing up his chest. "She is a fine lady and –and I'm just a bound man with three years yet on my contract before I can even make claim on any land or property, let alone to an honest suit for a lady of her station."

The little man laughed like a wild thing, his whole body vibrating with the joy of it. "Property don't make a gentleman," Mac Cuill said. "It's in the cut of his cloth and the straightness of his spine. The thickness of his blood and the sharpness o' the cast of his eyes. I see a ragged garment before me with a bit of a bend to him at the moment."

"Sirah!" Tommy exclaimed. "You are insulting me."

"See, there is hope," the little interloper noted. "You're not a complete shame to your mother—you can figure out the obvious when it is said out straight."

This statement was too much for the young man and he raised his hand to strike at the little man but as he did a glimmer of sunlight slashed across the room, perhaps some reflection from a belt buckle or glass jar but it was so bright the boy had to shield his eyes.

When Tommy could see again the little man was gone and the boy was once again alone in the room with the carved trunk! As much as he searched for minutes after, he could neither find where the man had come from nor to where had gone!

CHAPTER FIVE

KNIGHT IN THE NIGHT

Delinn Blayde had a full meal of venison and wild rice, a tankard of ale and went off to the stables where he made a nest of hay for himself in one of the lofts. There he slept deeply and woke naturally, well after moon fall, feeling fully rested and refreshed.

He had packed the wound in his side with a fresh poultice and stretched to test the extent of his recovery.

Good enough, he thought with barely a tinge of pain. *No reason to be lingering around here all day, I'll start to be mistaken for a lazy city man.*

He had resupplied his powder and shot, packed some jerky and pemmican with his sculpting tools in his sidepack and topped off his canteen before sleeping. It allowed him to simply slip out the back of the stable and head into the forest. He moved through the woods paralleling the trail toward Fort Pitt without being seen by the two guards that were supposed to be protecting the compound.

Sure, hope the guards are looking harder at the woods then in here at the compound, he thought. *Don't make me feel all that secure that they didn't notice a fella as big as me.*

+++

"Now keep your steps light, ya damn heathen," Bear Collins swore softly at Machk. "We can't afford to rouse any of these shopkeepers from their slumber; we don't have enough men for a face to face with this crew."

The Huron glared at the ursine felon but said nothing. The two men were crouched on a small rise overlooking the Van Stuben Inn complex. The moon had set, and the night was cold, dark and damp.

They had been watching the buildings all evening and Bear had waited until the tall scout Blayde had slipped away in advance of the morning sun, headed up the trail to look for another ambush.

"Looking for us," Collins laughed. "I knew he'd head out to scout, he's gonna be looking harder after tomorrow— if he is alive, come the day."

"I send three to follow him," the Huron leader said. "They watch until the time is good, then they make sure he does not come back."

"Good." The renegade white gave a satisfied smile. "You'll be a general yet, eh?"

Again, the red man merely stared at the ruffian, but his eyes were hooded his expression frozen and stoic.

"You and Penhat slip in and get the girl," Bear directed. "She's in that corner room. It will be easy to get in and out. The rest of us will stay spread out here and cover you. Remember, no noise and no looting. We have to get clean away if we are to make old man O'Rourke pay up what we want."

"Why you hate this man so much?" the Indian leader asked.

Being questioned shocked Collins and then he smiled. "That righteous old codger cheated me on a trapline deal because he said I was not high born enough to be dealt with like a 'gentleman.' He had me thrown out of his mansion; said I was unkempt." His eyes narrowed, he spit then gave a dark laugh. "I'll make him and Blayde both pay. Both of them will regret ever crossing Bear Collins for the rest of their miserable lives, which may not be all that long, come to think of it!"

Machk looked at Penhat with dark expressions but neither Huron said anything before slipping soundlessly off into the night, knives in hand.

+++

Tommy Mahoney couldn't sleep. He tossed and turned on the pile of straw in one of the out-buildings of the compound where the bondsmen slept, a tattered blanket wrapping around him like a shroud.

He kept replaying his odd conversation with the little man who called himself Nin Mac Cuill and each time there seemed to be fewer answers that made any sense. Tommy had searched the whole of the compound asking after the little man but no one, not Shamus, Maeve or any of the staff that had come along on the train knew anything of him. And none of the regular staff at the waystation knew anything of him. It made no sense.

A thief? Tommy thought, *But what did he steal? And why suddenly reveal himself with me there?* The question plagued him until he finally sat up in frustration.

The other servants in the out-building were snoring on the floor of the shed so the boy had to walk gingerly to make his way to the entrance without disturbing any of them.

Outside the night was almost pitch dark, the starlight of the moonless heavens providing faint illumination. Tommy stood for a time to let his eyes adjust then moved across the courtyard toward the main building with careful, measured steps.

Who was the little man? He kept repeating in his mind. *And what did he want?*

Tommy soon found himself standing across from the window of Mary O'Rourke's room before he realized it. He watched her darkened window, imagining her sleeping form inside. He felt embarrassed yet he smiled at the thought of her safe and snug within.

He played over her conversation with him from the afternoon, each word a song sung like a hymn in his memory. But try as he might to keep his mind on Mary he kept returning to the little man and that disturbed Tommy.

Maybe the little fella was right, he thought as he imagined her angelic form in repose. *Maybe somehow, I'm good enough; I mean I did fight that red Indian.* He imagined Mary's easy breathing and the perfect skin of her radiant face relaxed into a gentle slumber. He knew her long eyelashes would be fluttering as she dreamed.

Would she dream of me? He dared to think and smiled at the notion. *But such a thing is more than a bondman like me can hope.*

The smile vanished from his face as the window opened and a figure began to climb out! It was not distinct in the darkness, but it was definitely not Mary O'Rourke.

He had a sudden pang of jealousy and then reproached himself for churlishness when a second shape came out the window, but this one was not climbing out of its own accord. Instead, the figure was being handed out like a bit of baggage. The whole scenario sent a chill up the boy's spine; something was very, very wrong!

As before in the woods before he realized it, Tommy was in motion, quietly racing toward the dark shapes. He could find no voice to yell for help— in truth he still was uncertain what he was seeing, it could have been the wrong room and he was just witnessing some chicanery unrelated to the object of his affections.

By the time Tommy was close enough to see who the first dark figure was, he discovered to his horror that it was a Huron. Worse, the red man held the bound and gagged form of Mary O'Rourke in his arms! The girl's eyes were wide with terror. Then she saw Tommy approaching. The boy would remember her pleading look the rest of his life.

Tommy lunged forward and made a grab for the shoulder of the native who had the girl, almost reaching him, but abruptly a third figure appeared around the corner of the building. Suddenly Thomas Mahoney found himself embroiled in a life-or-death scuffle with a third Indian.

The boy tried to cry out now, sure that it was his only hope, but a hand like a steel vice grabbed him around the throat. The boy was forced to the ground under the weight of the Huron warrior leader Machk.

Tommy clawed wildly at the dark shape above him as he felt his wind being choked off. He was only vaguely aware of the other form now carrying Mary off, or of yet another figure that climbed out from the window, closing it behind them. The new figure spoke a few guttural words and then stepped in to bring a warclub down on young Mahoney's head.

Fireworks exploded inside the boy's head, and he had time for only one thought before he fell into absolute darkness. "Mary!"

+++

"Wake up, you worthless lummox," a reed thin voice said from out of the darkness of unconsciousness to Tommy Mahoney. "Come on, boyo, times a wasting and the blackguards are in the wind!" The shrill voice commanded,

"Open your lazy eyes and shake a leg, boyo!"

Tommy had to force his heavy lids to part. When he did, he was greeted by the sight of an angry Nin Mac Cuill backlit by the stars. At first the boy wondered why he was looking at the red bearded man then the memory of his battle with the Wyandot roared back into his mind and he gasped, "Miss O'Rourke!"

"Well at least you have your priorities straight, laddie. Even if your puny muscles did the poor girl little or no good."

Tommy sat up too quickly and his head began to spin. When he focused his eyes on the little man again, he gasped, "I've had my head split open and I'm dying. I'm seeing things!"

It was the only explanation for what appeared before his eyes; the man in the odd green jacket seated cross-legged, but it that appeared Mac Cuill was floating several feet off the ground.

"Mary," Tommy whispered her name as if it was a prayer and a cry for help. "We have to tell the others; she's been taken by the Wyandots!"

"Those fools will be as useless as you were, boyo," the little man said. "At least as useless as you were before I came to tutor you!"

The way he spoke, the tone, not the words frightened young Mahoney as nothing else about the whole strange night had not. The little man waved his hands, and the motion drew Tommy's attention.

They were like the motions of a puppeteer pulling strings, heaving himself up to his feet as if pulled by ropes. He shook his head to clear it, sure he was still dizzy from the blow and tried to resist the compulsion to stand at the little man's command.

"What are you doing?" Tommy stammered.

Nin Mac Cuill smiled and floated over the back of the boy. "How is simple as you are, boyo," he said. "How it is that I am a spirit of the old sod bound by time and choice to the oak that trunk was fashioned from. And why? Well, aside from not likin' the kind of brutal shenanigans in general that could bring harm the helpless lasses such as the lovely Mary, I have been bound to the Family O'Rourke by pact and honor for many generations." He gave a little wink. "And the gal, like her ancestors, has the sight, you know. Like you do, as well, by the way, boyo."

Tommy barely listened to the words the little man spoke as he tried to fight the little man's weird control over him. He tried to yell for help, but his voice would not obey him. He looked at the floating Mac Cuill and repeated, "What are you doing to me?"

"Makin' you useful, boyo," Mac Cuill said. "I would be chargin' off and savin' the lass meself but I do hate to walk; some might suppose it's me advanced age, but truth be told I've just gotten smarter as time has gone on."

...a hand like a steel vice grabbed him around the throat.

As he spoke the little man floated over the back of Mahoney and suddenly 'dropped' onto the boy's shoulders.

Tommy shook his head in confusion, as if to deny what was happening to him. Here, before him was a thing that could not be yet here it was, a pagan remnant of the past. It was a creature out of the tales his grandma would tell him, actually one of the little people—a Fae! It was enough to make a good Christian like Tommy think he had been cursed!

"Now get up and movin' like an oat eatin' reprobate, consider yerself press-ganged," the little man commanded the bondsman. "We've got a bit of white knightin' to be doin!"

Tommy had no choice but to comply with the not so gentle kick in the ribs from the little man's heels and move forward into the night.

The strange pair moved out into the darkness of the woods so that the sound of Tommy's booted feet was deadened by the thick carpet of dermis on the floor of the forest. In fact, all sound seemed to be swallowed up as the unusual pair entered the tree line.

"Now then," the little man resting on Tommy's shoulders whispered. "We have to find where the heathen devils have taken the fair damsel." He made a humming sound and added. "Maybe I should have turned you into an actual hound, eh, boyo, so you could sniff them out? I did say the girl needed her own Cuchulainn, eh?"

Tommy tried to answer the little man, but his voice was only a hoarse whisper. "Let me go…"

"You do want to help the lass, now, don't you boyo?"

"Yes."

"Then quiet while a master woodsman with a nose for tracking does his very best to locate the fair lady, eh? Ye can best serve in silence."

With a brittle laugh and a low whistle, the strange man put heel to Tommy's side and drove the two of them further into the woods.

I am either going insane, Tommy thought, *or I will run directly into the savages who stole Mary. That'll make sure they can kill me, take my hair, not help her at all*!

CHAPTER SIX

RELATIVE CALM?

It seemed to the press-ganged Tommy that they were just wandering aimlessly through the woods until they came to a large oak tree.

The false dawn was painting the horizon pink as Nin Mac Cuill 'dismounted' the confused bondsman to leave Tommy standing befuddled while he casually walked to the large trunk of the tree.

The little, green-coated Mac Cuill went directly to the gnarled tree and to Tommy's amazement the little man simply knocked on the trunk as if asking entrance to some secret haunt.

Three times in a steady rhythm the little man struck while humming a tune; knock, knock, knock.

He repeated this strange ritual several times and then stepped back with his hands on his hips. He cocked his head to the side and hummed a melody with an expectant attitude.

Mac Cuill's expression became annoyed when nothing happened right away and so he stepped forward again just as a strange figure stepped from behind the lee of the massive oak.

It was hunched figure, even smaller than the Irish Fae with long wild black hair and whose near naked form was covered with moss and hanging greenery. Most remarkable was the face of the apparition, it was a twisted mockery of a human visage with two unevenly spaced eyes and a twisted mouth and hooked nose.

At first Tommy thought it was a mask such as Declinn had said the Indians carved from the living trees, but then the apparition's eyes blinked, and it spoke with the naturalness of a living being's face.

"Why have you summoned Achak?"

"Greetings, cousin," Nin Mac Cuill said with a wide smile. He abruptly had a long clay pipe in his hand, and he took a puff on it. He blew out a long plume of smoke into the face of the stranger then held the pipe out to offer it to the gnomish figure before him. "Nin Mac Cuill of the *Dannian Sidhe* at your service, I greet you with a brother's great joy."

The wild figure of Achak took the offered pipe, took a puff and returned it to the green clad Irishman after blowing smoke back at the red head. The smoke curled around them both to hang like a joint cloak.

"Have you come to invade our woods as well like the pale humans, brother spirit?" the odd faced figure asked.

"Not by a half, Cousin," the Irish Fae said. "I was an unwilling passenger on this trip, nonetheless I have obligations that have bound me to those pale folk who live here now. I apologize for any shenanigans those pale folk have done."

The little wildman with the twisted face gave his version of a grin that was chilling. "How may Achak serve his spirit brother?"

"Well, this may be a bit much," the green clad Fae said. "It seems I've mislaid a young colleen I feel honor bound to be protecting and I'd like you help me to find her."

The twist-faced spirit nodded his head. "I know of the squaw you seek: Huron who consort with whiteskins and who do not respect the old ways have taken her."

"Well, there you, see, boyo," Mac Cuill addressed Tommy. "We Fae are a lot more civilized than you mortals sorts."

The captive Mahoney could still manage some speech and he half whined a response. "We have to save her!"

"Well, you awful looking lad," the little man laughed. "That is something, at least, that we can all agree on!"

+++

When Declinn Blayde left the German's Inn long before daylight it was at his usual steady run despite the darkness. He planned to put considerable distance along the road to Fort Pitt before the sun rose. His side didn't bother him anymore after what he considered a luxurious full day of rest.

The woodsman still had that 'odd feeling' there would be trouble and so, even with Shamus telling him otherwise, he went on ahead intending to look for signs of another ambush. He was sure the trouble was not over yet. By sunrise he was already miles up the trail having found no sign of trouble, but the feeling of impending danger was still just as strong.

Dangdest thing, he thought as he sat for a moment's rest and a sip of water on a rise overlooking the trail ahead. *That prickling feeling in the back of my neck just keeps getting worse.*

He let himself relax against a tree just enough to feel the slight ache in his side from his wound.

I must be getting old, he thought with a wry smile. *For such a little pinprick to bother me this long.* He sipped from his water flask again and fixed his gaze on the road to the fort.

It was a mistake, for the three Indian's that had followed him were moving up stealthily behind him with murder in their eyes and tomahawks in their hands…

+++

Mary O'Rourke was carried like so much baggage into the depths of the woods. She had awakened only when the two Wyandot warriors had seized her, a callused hand clamped over her mouth before she could scream. Her struggle had been brief, until a glancing blow from a warclub had rocked her back into near slumber. As she slipped in and out of consciousness, she saw the Indians strike the still sleeping Maeve.

The girl only prayed the old servant woman was still alive. Then as the girl found herself, still dazed, being hauled out the window, seeing Tommy struck down had only deepened Mary's sense of hopelessness. And seeing the brave lad clubbed had also affected her in a way she would not have expected, awakening emotions she had not realized she had for him.

When Mary's struggle had been renewed, she was struck again and this time into full unconsciousness.

Mary expected to be killed. The girl was sure she was in the hands of the devil himself and so was shocked when she was jostled awake to find herself draped over the shoulder of the muscular brave that carried her. She tried to cry out, but a crude gag jammed into her mouth muffled all her protests.

Now the girl, exhausted from her fright, and her struggles stayed limp but watchful. The muscular savage carried her on seemingly tireless legs through the impenetrable darkness of the forest. Her captors had not spoken but she gained the impression from their progress that they were intent on a particular destination.

Her suspicion was proven true when her carrier rounded a thicket of brush and came on a ramshackle camp where a dozen more Indian warriors sat waiting.

What shocked her more than the kidnapping had, however, was the figure in the center of the camp that met the runner.

"So, you got the wench, eh, Machk?" A mountain of a white man asked. "Any trouble?"

The brute that was carrying Mary set her down roughly and grunted. "Too noisy!"

"You— you're a white man?" She exclaimed in shock after she ripped the gag from her mouth. "How could you be a part of this? Why in Heaven's name have you done this?"

Bear Collins stepped forward and snapped a thick hand out to slap the girl across the cheek with such force that she was thrown to the ground.

"I'll take no back talk from you, you spoiled, skinny tart!" the towering Collins said. "If you speak up again, I'll ask one of the Hurons to find a better way to keep you quiet than that gag!"

The girl made a strangled sound but stopped herself from hurling the invectives she was thinking. Instead, she only glared at the bandit chief and ground her teeth, tasting blood from where she bit the inside of her mouth when he hit her.

Her expression made Collins laugh. "That's right, missy. You just think all the terrible thoughts you want about poor old Bear, but you keep them to yourself. I thunk that and a lot more about your father when he cast me out like I was just a filthy animal. Now he will think about old Bear a whole lot when he gets the note Machk left. He'll think about me all the time from this day forward. Every day, reckon." He laughed again, louder at the quiet tears the girl shed at his boast.

+++

Tommy Mahoney had never felt more humiliated in his life. He had been forced to carry both Nin Mac Cuill and the twist-faced native spirit on his two shoulders through the forest.

The odd trio was moving along an animal track deep in the woods with brush scrapping against Tommy's sides, scratching the arms he attempted to fend the branches off with. Adding insult to it all flies had already decided to feast on him as if he were a real mount.

This is horrible, he thought as he loped along at the behest of the Irish Fae.

"Move along, you lazy gadabout, put on some speed," the redhaired Fae chided. "We have a damsel to save." He laughed and his long-haired fellow spirit gave a very un-ghostly giggle.

"Big dog is best way for white men to be," Achak laughed. His twisted mouth gave his voice an unusual two-toned sound, like a wind instrument blown with too much power. "Maybe I learn spell from Brother Mac Cuill and change all invaders into real dogs."

"Oh, I've thought about doing that to the darned English for a century," the Irish Fae said. "But I had word from the fairy council in a very firm form that told me I couldn't be so—uh- high handed I believe they called it."

The native spirit grunted, if it were really possible, and made an annoyed face that distorted his features even more. "Manitou Elder Council tell me same thing: 'medicine only to be used in 'case by case basis."

The Irish Fae produced a small flask from beneath his green coat and handed it back to the false-faced Fae. The little native spirit took a sip, grunted again and then threw back a deep drink.

"Not all white inventions bad," Achak said with a rasping tone. "This much better than the *Pulque* of the Aztecs or *Balche* of the Maya. I like it."

"Good old Whiskey, boyo cousin," Mac Cuill said. "The very reason the Irish haven't conquered the world yet—might be best to worship at its altar in moderation."

The native Fae just grunted again.

Tommy continued to move along the narrow, trackless trail. It was a path that was little more than a slightly wide space between the undergrowth. His eyesight was poor in the dense overgrowth even in the growing daylight. He realized he was sweating profusely and thought that he must have a pretty heavy scent at that point.

Yet the only scent I want to smell is Mary's perfume, the 'captive' bondsman thought. With that thought, despite being cruelly used by the two wood spirits Tommy increased his speed and pressed forward. *I will save her*, he thought. *I have to!*

+++

Declinn Blayde could not shake the sense of 'wrongness' that had followed him for most of the morning's run. He closed his leather water skin and took out a knife to whittle a small piece of wood he'd found along the trail. He settled back to watch the trail again as the sun worked its way up through the trees.

He had taken the scouting job for the O'Rourke party as an excuse to visit his sister Deirdre who had moved to live with the family of her brother-in-law, Stewart Collins. Declinn had not seen her in months since her husband's death in the Willow Creek Massacre and thought it would be an easy trip. That massacre had made the sculptor more conscious of the need to keep in contact.

I should listen to my own advice to young Mahoney, he thought, *not everything is what it appears to be.*

In just a few strokes of his blade the stick he was whittling began to take crude shape as a wolf's head. The carving relaxed him and sometimes helped him think more clearly and he was hoping it would help him focus on the reason for his misgivings about the trail.

I think that attack was too well put together for them to abandon the O'Rourke's train after only one try. The question is when and where will they make another attempt?

After a few minutes he was just about to rise to head back along the trail when that tingling at the back of his neck became so strong that he turned to look back toward the inn.

He was just in time to see the tomahawk of the first Huron brave coming at his face!

CHAPTER SEVEN

MASKED AND TASKED

Tommy Mahoney moved along at a better speed once the sun was up, burning off the morning mist and warming the woods. That only freed his mind to think about poor Mary's fate with even more concern.

Tommy had heard the talk of what the savage Wyandot or their Iroquois enemy had done to prisoners during the last war, and he shuddered with the thought.

"Mary!" he whispered out loud. The picture of the girl with the red hands of the natives on her pale flesh made the boy's blood boil. He suddenly found more strength in his stride, and he pushed forward with a new burst of speed.

"Oh, the Hound of Cullian has the scent, eh?" Mac Cuill said with a chuckle.

"Uh,' Achak said. "I think white big dog just has a hungry belly."

It was then that Tommy realized he did scent food; someone not too far ahead on the trail was cooking a wood hen. He concentrated and he could smell the cooking meat clearly. Then an errant gust of wind brought the smell he knew so well. *Mary's perfume!*

He had often recalled that sweet smell as he lay on his bare pallet at night; a fresh, joyous scent that was all flowers and all sunshine to him. He grunted with annoyance at the scent and tried to move even faster.

"Whoa, big fella," the Fae on his right shoulder said. Mac Cuill pulled on Tommy's long hair like a rein. "We can't just go blundering in there; these are practically English thugs!"

"Hey!" Achak said.

"Sorry," the Irish spirit said, "No offense meant, me cuz—but you have to admit these fellows are rotters."

"I need to save her!" Tommy uttered in a hoarse whisper "Please!"

"Well, that is the spirit," the Irish Fae said. "And that is why I brought you along, besides me having a considerable dislike of walking."

Mac Cuill hopped off Tommy's shoulder while the native Fae leapt upward to scurry up the side of a tree to hang upside down from a branch like a bat.

"But we just can't just go rushing in there, we have to use stealth, boyo. I may be able to avoid one of those heathen arrows…" he looked up at Achak and said, "No offense." Then Mc Cuill continued, "But you are pure decay flesh if you get one of them stuck in you!"

Tommy pushed forward through the screen of leaves that skirted the edge of a small clearing. There he froze, ahead were the prey he had been chasing.

There were nearly a dozen figures lounging around the clearing almost all of them Huron warriors. One was a large white man wearing a thick fur coat and beside him, looking all the smaller for his size was the beautiful object of Tommy's passion, Mary O'Rourke.

+++

The tomahawk slammed into the tree close enough to Declinn Blayde's head to pin some of his hair to the trunk. The Wyandot followed it in a heartbeat, but Blayde already had his knife out to whittle so he was able to thrust it directly into the brave's chest.

The attacker dropped at Declinn's feet but before Blayde could withdraw the knife or reach for his rifle a second warrior was on him. That brave collided with Declinn with enough force to drive the wind out of his lungs.

The woodsman was forced to clamp his arms around the Wyandot to keep the Indian from using his tomahawk, but it left him trapped against the tree. The third warrior came on at a fast run with a warclub raised but his companion being held by Declinn inhibited him from getting a clear swing at the frontiersman.

The third Indian warrior yelled in his native language to the captured brave to get out of the way, but Blayde made sure he could not do that. Instead, the woodsman put a foot against the tree trunk and pushed off with all his might. This propelled both him and the Wyandot into the third warrior, ripping some of Blayde's hair in the process.

The three of them hit the ground, but just before they did Declinn released his prisoner, so that when they slammed into the dirt the frontiersman rolled free. He was too far from his rifle to make a move for it, so the woodsman pulled a wood mallet and a steel chisel from his sculpting tools in his side pack.

The two braves quickly regained their footing and charged at Blayde, splitting to approach from each side in hopes of overwhelming him. They had not reckoned with the fact that the sculptor had spent countless hours with the mallet in his hand, often juggling it while he considered a curve or line to alter.

As the brave on his left lunged in, Declinn launched the mallet with perfect accuracy, hitting the brave between the eyes hard enough to lift him off the ground. The strike hit with a cracking sound like a gunshot.

The second brave was on Declinn in an instant and the brave drove a knife into Blayde's side at the same moment that the woodsman jammed the chisel through the eye socket of the Wyandot, killing him.

Done it this time, Blayde he thought as he rolled off the body of the dead Indian. *Not gonna be good to anyone after this.*

Then the woodsman shuddered and passed out from pain and loss of blood!

+++

The sight of the Mary O'Rourke in the clearing made Tommy's heart race and he started to push his way through the bush, but the small hand of Mac Cuill grabbed tight on his arm. The touch of the little Fae actually froze

Tommy so that he could not move.

"Don't be impetuous, boyo," Mac Cuill whispered. "You're no Cuhullian yet; we've got to be sneaky as a British barrister!"

"Sneaky!" Tommy hissed. He thought of Declinn and his ability to move through the woods unseen and unheard and felt more horribly inadequate than usual.

Tommy stared back at the little man. "Why do I have to sneak?" he managed to snort at the edge of desperation. "You can make yourself disappear, right? So why can't you do that for me?"

"That is providence of me own folk," the little Irish Fae said. "I can't be given you that ability, boyo! The thought of a mortal being able to blink in and out, that's no telling what mischief would happen!"

Tommy tried to pull away from the little man's hand but still had no movement. A sudden inspiration hit the boy. "Why not use a spell of some sort and disguise me in some way?"

The Irish Fae considered the statement and then smiled. "Why, sure as you are just that now, you useful piece of flesh! It's a glimmer spell you're talking about and that shows you have some glimmer of a wit about you." He patted the boy on the hip. "If you're to be the Hound of Ulster for the maid, it's only fitting that you look the part!"

Tommy stared at him with little or no idea what the Fae was saying, a fact made plain by his expression. Mac Cuill snorted. "I can't be changin' you into a hound, boyo, or I'll catch all from the elders; but I can make you *look* like a ruddy great dog to those feathered hooligans! Then you can just wander in there and get up close to the girl and be ready for whatever happens."

Tommy frowned not really liking liked the idea of being turned into an animal or even looking like one. Then he thought of how long it would take to find his way back to the Inn to get help to save Mary and said, "Alright, then, do what you must!"

"Not all that easy, boyo," the Irish spirit said. "I'm not on me home ground now, ya know, and well, I'm not at me best in all." He frowned. "But I think with me cousin's help we might be able to fool these fellas." He looked up at the false-faced spirit who swung from one branch to the other before squatting on one to look down at the two.

"Ugh—" the Iroquois spirit said. "Pretty big joke on Huron dogs for sure." He flexed his short legs then jumped down soundlessly from the tree. "Let's do!"

He and the Irish Fae began to mumble in a language so old all fairy folk spoke it and soon a small ball of light was formed between the two.

Tommy crossed himself and called on every saint he knew by name as he watched the two Fae cast their spell. He looked away from them to glance back at the clearing where Mary was being held to bolster his resolve to even try even the outrageous idea of using magic to save her.

"Okay, boyo," Nin Mac Cuill said with a sly smile on his face. "Remember you'll just look like a hound to those devil's out there; don't go thinking you are big and strong as one!"

"Hey, you don't have to make fun of me while you humiliate me!"

"Bah!" Achak said. "White men all weak." He looked over at Mac Cuill and added, "No offense meant."

The Irish Fae frowned but ignored the statement to gesture, sending the glowing ball of energy toward Tommy.

The bluish light enveloped the boy from head to foot.

"That's it?" Tommy asked as he looked at his hands and arms unchanged. "It didn't work."

The two Fae shook their heads.

"Why you pick this one?" Achak asked Mac Cull, "He seem not to be much right in head."

"Well, and sure I did not pick him for his brains, Cousin," the Irishman said. "But the lass fancies his look, at least."

"You're just making fun of me and it's not fair." Tommy insisted. "I just want to help Mary."

Mac Cuill pulled a looking glass that was impossibly too big to have been under his coat and held it up for Tommy to see.

The boy was startled to see a great wolfhound looking back at him from the mirror.

"Now get in there and get the girl like a real Red Branch hero." Mac Cuill said. "Before you embarrass your matter, patter and me further!"

CHAPTER EIGHT

A HOUND HEROIC

Tommy decided that his best course of action was to win sympathy for his canine impersonation, so he slunk into the clearing with his head down and did his best to whine like a wounded hound.

The braves in the clearing all leapt to their feet as the hound broke through the underbrush. He whimpered, lowered his head and walked directly across the open space to stand next to the bound girl and nuzzled her with his long nose.

"Where did you come from, fella?" she said with a giggle.

Bear Collins was right beside her with a pistol in hand and scanned the woods where Tommy had come from.

"Get into the trees," the bandit chief commanded the braves. "They may have followed us from the Inn."

The Huron braves all scattered, and Collins kept his eyes out toward the edge of the clearing.

Mary looked to the forest as well, so she was startled when the whispered voice of Tommy Mahoney came to her.

"Take heart, Miss O'Rourke," the hound-disguised boy said. "You are not alone anymore."

The girl looked around with wonderment, her eyes staring past the canine figure that stood next to her.

She really doesn't know it's me! Tommy thought. *And why should she?* He suddenly felt how horribly strange it all was. He felt so terribly vulnerable standing in the center of the clearing full of armed men. He had no real idea what to do next.

No, I am here, miss, Tommy whispered as he nuzzled his massive head into her shoulder. Her scent was heady and the touch of her skin to his nose sent a different kind of chill coursing through him. He set about working the ropes that bound her wrists behind her back, but the knots were intricate.

"What?" the girl now looked directly into his eyes that stared down at her. There was a moment where there was disbelief and then a recognition that the hound had actually spoken to her.

"Master Mahoney?" She whispered.

He shook his head up and down in agreement. Her eyes widened with acknowledgement, and she mouthed 'how?"

Collins stepped up close to the girl again and grabbed her shoulder. "Come with me, missy," he said. "I don't like this at all, no sir, not at all."

Seeing the big man put a hand on Mary's shoulder enraged the canine Mahoney and he darted forward to head butt Bear.

Collins was so startled by the violent action that he fell over sideways more from surprise than force.

"Up and run, miss," Tommy said. He half pulled her to her feet by grasping her shoulders.

Mary sprang up as quickly as she could with her hands still tied and with loosely bound feet would allow. She allowed Tommy to propel her forward as Collins pulled himself to his feet.

"Run!" Tommy insisted as he spun to face the brigand.

Bear pointed his flintlock at the fleeing 'hound' and girl and pulled the hammer back.

+++

The Huron warriors raced into the brush ready to face a full -fledged attack from the German's Inn but were met instead by a wall of green and an unearthly silence. None of the night creatures moved or sounded in the woods.

"This is wrong," Machk said to the brave to his right. "There is bad medicine here!"

Almost as if it had been a cue to call down the wrath of the woods an army of small beast: squirrels, shrews, mice, rabbits, ferrets, deer and birds exploded out of the darkness at the warriors, overwhelming them with sudden chittering and squealing attacks. All the warriors were knocked over and born to the ground.

"Nicely done," Nin Mac Cuill laughed to the native spirit Achak.

The wild haired native spirit grunted. "This just the start." He waved a gourd rattle and the wall of green now erupted with the bodies of the predators that had been chasing the prey game. Puma, bear, fox, coyote, owls, lynx and bobcats sprang from the darkness with fire in their eyes.

These beasts did not merely run over the fallen braves, they fell on the human warriors with ravenous snarls and roars.

"It is not the way of The People to take women," the native tree spirit said with bitterness, "Or to serve an invading devil."

"I hope you're not putting me in that category, cousin?" Mac Cuill frowned.

The twisted faced spirit made his ugly features into the semblance of a grin. "You are a guest; they are the ones who invade."

"Well, you're welcome to a jolly time if yeh ever decide to head over to the Old Sod. And we have an endless supply of the whiskey back home."

Bear Collins took careful aim at the fleeing girl determined to keep his prize from escaping him at all costs. He reasoned he could still ransom her corpse as long as her father didn't know she was dead. As he leveled the flintlock it exploded out of his hand just a moment before Tommy slammed into the greasy kidnapper.

Tommy snarled and cursed and pounded his fists against the massive body of Collins, trying to keep the kidnapper down but the brute merely grabbed the 'hound' that was on him and flung it off like he was discarding an old coat.

Tommy landed hard, feeling a great rushing wind and a tingle that made him aware that the spell was leaving his form. He rolled over onto his back with a moan prepared to accept an attack from Bear in time to see Declinn Blayde stagger from the woods at a stumbling run.

"It ain't polite to point, Bear," the tall woodsman said as he set his smoking long rifle aside that he had used to shoot the pistol out of Bear's hand. Declinn leaned against a tree, his eyes locked with Bears. His buckskin jacket was stained a deep, dark red.

He paused and slipped a tomahawk from his belt. "I back tracked the three vermin you sent to do me harm, Bear, and cut across young Tom's trail thinking it was more your sort followed it back here."

The tall woodsman looked over at the fallen boy. "You done good, Tommy, now get that girl of yours home." When Tommy's stunned expression, he added, "Go ahead, it's time for me to finish with Bear Collins here. It's what I should have done in that tavern a coupla years back."

"You ain't man enough to finish nothin'," Collins yelled as he drew his own long knife.

Tommy rolled to his feet and was torn between going to help Blayde and taking Mary home. One look at the confused expression on the girl's face as her gaze went from him to Blayde and he knew he had to get to her.

"Master Mahoney," she gasped when he reached her. "What is going on, I saw you—I mean—I thought—"

"Hush, miss," the boy gently took her arm, "You're still a bit confused from the ordeal, let us get you home and to safety." He managed to get her into the woods while he worked on the ropes that held her arms. He only took time for a quick backward glance just as Collins charged Blayde.

The two frontiersmen collided like forces of nature. They slammed together, blades flashing in the night. The men grappled, each grabbing the weapon hand of the other then fell to the ground, still locked. They rolled end over end through the clearing scattering the campfire as they rolled through it like a small tornado.

Bear cursed and roared in anger, but Blayde was eerily silent, his face a mask of concentration while the two wrestled. Or was that pain?

At the edge of the clearing Tommy once more hesitated, thinking for a moment of running back to help the scout. Then heard a whispered voice that seemed to come from directly above him.

"The mighty man's just fine, boyo," Mac Cuill called from a tree branch where he sat. "Get the lass back to her folks at the Inn."

Tommy knew it was probably the best thing to do, but seeing the woodsman locked in conflict with the monstrous Collins tugged at his conscience.

He finally got the ropes on Mary free but stopped for a moment.

"Miss O'Rourke," he said with a serious tone. "I want nothing more to take you all the way back to the inn myself, but I can't leave Master Blayde to continue the battle himself, you could see he was wounded."

"But Master Mahoney how will I—"

"Mac Cuill," Tommy called out to the girl's amazement, "you'll have to be the one to get her back."

At the mention of his name the little Fae popped out from behind a tree.

"Now don't be leaving a job half done," the Fae said. "Save the damsel, ye half hound, ye!"

Mary looked stunned at the sudden appearance of the remarkable little man but before she could question further Tommy interjected.

"I am sorry, sir, but I cannot desert a comrade in need." He started to head back then, stopped, turned to the girl and said, "If I don't come back, Miss Mary—I—uh—you are so—*oh tarnation!*" then he whirled and raced back into the clearing.

"Ah," Mac Cuill, said with a shrug, "One cannot fault heart over brains, can one, lass?"

Mary looked down at him with a confused expression as he bowed and added, "Allow me to introduce meself…"

+++

Declinn Blayde was in a bad way.

Bear Collins was in full rage and power, and he was using his massive hands to bludgeon the wounded woodsman while they grappled. He kept pounding on Declinn's bleeding side where he had a knife wound. The constant pain of it was keeping Blayde from being able to retaliate, indeed, to be able to concentrate at all.

Tommy charged into the clearing with a defiant war cry and launched himself onto Collin's back. It was as if he were tackling a buffalo. He might as well have been, for though he latched onto the bearskin pelt on the massive kidnapper his weight was barely noticed by the savage Bear.

"I'll smash you to jelly," Collins growled at Blayde, "then I'll tear your dog of a whelp apart in front of you."

Somehow being called 'a dog' infuriated Tommy even more than anything else the kidnapper might have said. The boy used the pelt on the coat to climb forward on the man's massive back till he was at Collin's shoulders. Then Tommy reached around Bear's head to claw at the man's eyes with both hands.

Collins screamed in annoyance at the attack and was forced to stop striking at Blayde to reach back and grab at Mahoney.

That pause in the assault was all that Declinn needed to rally himself and he heaved to the side which rolled both Bear and Tommy off of him.

Bear landed partially on Tommy that caused the boy to gasp out in pain. But he kept his fingers curled and scratching at Bear's eyes with terrier tenacity.

Declinn climbed to his knees with a roar of defiance and yelled, "Here,

...flung it off like he was discarding an old coat.

Bear, come get justice!" This was just at the moment that Collins caught Tommy's wrists that yanked him off his back, tossing the boy to the ground with exaggerated violence.

"I'll gut you," Collin's screamed in reply to the scout. He rolled to his knees and pulled a tomahawk from his belt. He swung the weapon at Blayde, but the scout pulled his own. The two weapons collided with sparks and a sound like contained thunder.

Blayde pushed himself off from his knees with a Herculean effort and rocketed into Bear, smashing his forehead into Collin's face, breaking his nose with a spray of blood.

Both men rolled to the ground again, but this time with Blayde on top and he fastened his long, strong fingers around Collin's thick throat. Bear's eye bulged and he tried to curse, but there was not enough air getting through.

He struggled and kicked, but Blayde's hands were workman's hands, sculptor's hands and their power— even with Declinn bleeding— was enough to crush the life out of the brigand.

When Collin's stopped moving Blayde blew out a hissing breath and fell over sideways himself.

"Master Blayde!" Tommy ran to the fallen man's side just as Mary O'Rourke came running out of the trees clutching a branch as a club.

"Tommy!" Mary called when she saw that the boy had been scratched and dirtied by the struggle and that he was smeared with blood. She did not know it was actually Declinn's. She ran to join the boy at the fallen Blayde's side and together with Tommy, worked to revive the fallen man.

Mac Cuill stepped from the trees with an exasperated expression on his face. "Stubborn," he said with hiss. "Just like so many back home."

"Mortals all stubborn!" The native false face Fae noticed.

"Aye," Mac Cuill agreed, "I think the ones from Eire are special sort of stubborn breed for sure—but I'll give it to them, they have more than their share of heart!"

+++

By the time Tommy and Mary O'Rourke got the wounded Blayde back to the inn half dragging, half carrying the tall scout the whole way, the complex was awake and frantic with recently discovered news of the kidnapping.

The note that had been left behind had demanded an exorbitant ransom and no one could decide exactly what to do with so outrageous a manifesto.

"My angel!" Old Maeve, her head bandaged, cried as she ran to Mary. The kidnapped girl walked beside a limping, near unconscious Blayde while Tommy acted as a living crutch to the tall woodsman. Blayde was so exhausted he could not even complain about needing the help.

Mary was scraped and with her hair matted but she was smiling "Tommy saved my life," the girl said with awe as some hot rum, bread and cheese were brought for her.

She filled in the pieces of the story that they did not know; that the Indians had stolen her at Bear's orders and sent some braves to ambush Blayde. Now, she added with an almost joyous finality, Bear and all his mean were dead.

She had already been convinced by Tommy that there should be no mention of the little man they had met in the woods. He made it clear that no one would believe her anyway and she was too tired and too elated to be rescued to question the Providence of the Fae's intervention any further.

In the courtyard Tommy held court for not only the other bondsmen, but for most of the rest of the inn. Mary sat nearby, against Mauve's admonishments and unabashedly smiled whenever the boy looked her way (which he did frequently).

Declinn sat quietly with his heavily bandaged side, sipping some single malt with Shamus as he watched the boy enjoy this new celebrity.

Nin Mac-Cuill, who perched on the edge of a rafter unseen by those below, spoke to Achak.

"Well, the boyo's gotten a better deal than he deserved." The little Irish Fae laughed with satisfaction, "What do you think, cousin?"

The tree spirit chuckled as well. "This one thinks that all dogs will howl when it is their day."

Tommy Mahoney had a hard time disagreeing when, each day after that, Mary would smile at him for many years to follow and indeed he became the Hound of O'Rourke.

THE LONG JOURNEY HOME

RAGNAR'S CURSE

The Skraeling horde
Had swarmed aboard
When they had stopped to rest,
Their knives were keen, their arrows red
As assault repeated
Pressed
But Ragnar cried
'We'll make them die!"
And rallied all his swords
To cut and hack
And force them back
And master all
The wards
Three days they
Fought
Friend and foe both fell
All were bloodied
Sent on point to
Hel
But Ragnar stood,
His head held high
And faced the charging swarm
While crimson
Painted enemies
Kept his axe blade warm
Till last alone
The Northman snarled
His blade with none
To slay
And cursed the Wyrd that meant
He would not drink
With Odin
On that day.

PROLOGUE

1,081 AD

Ragnar Longaxe was tired, more tired than he had ever been in his twenty-five years on Midgard.

It had been days since he had slept, almost that long since he'd anything but roots and berries to eat or rainwater to drink.

The Skraelings would not let him rest, harrying him and his brother's day and night as they drove the Northmen ahead of them. The savages pursued them relentlessly, driving them inland into the rugged hills of this new country, further and further away from the comforting ocean-sea and the sanctuary of their beached ship.

There had been full dozen of the armed Northmen when they left their longship hidden in a river berth to venture ashore. They planned to bury the plunder of a full season to retrieve later. Now only Ragnar and one other survived.

The captain of their vessel, Sven Bluetooth, was worried that the Swede's who they had raided would overtake them with the ship overloaded with their plunder. Sven decided to bury the loot inland and resupply with meat and fruits before returning home to get another ship and more men.

The land locked crew had been burdened with the plunder and so moved slowly. Ragnar, tallest and strongest of his brother warriors, with red beard and long copper colored hair flowing, could carry twice what any others could and laughed at them, calling them 'little boys' when they complained at the weight.

The seafaring group had soon come upon a village of the brown little Skraelings and, as was their way, the Northmen took what they wanted. They had their fill of food and consorted with the women whether they wanted it or not and had killed any of the men who objected.

The Northmen had dallied in the village for two days in the torpor brought on by lust and gluttony. That had been their mistake.

On the morning of the third day scores of little painted men swarmed out of the woods, charging them and launching a rain of arrows. Most of the crew were wounded but they were lucky that most were still dressed in their chainmail shirts and their metal helmets, their *spanghelms,* which were proof against all but a lucky missile shot.

The little screaming natives had no iron weapons, but their sheer numbers and the insane courage of continued attacks took its toll on the seafaring invaders, forcing the Northmen to grab their booty and retreat into the woods.

The Skraelings continued the attacks, pursuing the burdened crew day and night for days without a break.

One by one Ragnar's treasure laden brothers fell to the rocks, spears and arrow stings of the little painted men, until only Bjorn, called The Wise who shaved his face like an Englishman, and the redhaired Ragnar were left.

Now, in one of the periodic lulls in the relentless attacks, the giant Ragnar moved first while Bjorn followed, watching the underbrush with haunted eyes. Both men knew the Skraeling's numbers assured that there was no path back toward the ship the way they had come.

"The feathered trolls are still out there, Ragnar," Bjorn said. His voice was hoarse and strained. "I know it."

"So do I, brother." Ragnar still carried four men's burden of gold and jewels, pushing himself forward by force of will. "So why do you say it? It is their Wyrd to follow and ours to escape, I know it in my heart. We just have to get higher in the rocks; we can find a place to make a stand." The redhead's breath was ragged as the weight of the plunder, combined with the pace of their route was wearing on even his massive physique.

"We should just leave the cursed treasure and fight our way through to the ship," Bjorn said.

"Why anyone ever calls you 'wise', Odin knows. This treasure is King Olaf's by right. Sven Bluetooth swore to see it safe to him and we swore as well. Would you break your word on the oath ring and twist our Wyrd?"

"But—"

"But no!" Ragnar suddenly raged, new strength flowing into his powerful limbs at the resurrection of the argument the two men had been having for much of the day. "We are charged to keep this treasure and we shall! There is no argument."

The two paused to catch their breath, all the time scanning the dense woods around them. They knew their feathered foes must still lurk out there somewhere, just beyond their sight, but the painted ones had not attacked them for some time.

"Could they have given up on the hunt?" Bjorn hoped.

"No," his companion noted. "They have wolf's blood, and they scent us as easy prey now. They are just resting to ready another attack, I am sure."

Ragnar spat. "We will find a safe cave for this, bury it well and then we will cut our way through the damnable little men. We'll either join to the other few we left at the ship or our brothers in Valhalla!" He brandished the two-handed axe he had been leaning on as a walking stick to reinforce his point.

"As you say, Ragnar." The smaller man gave a wolfish grin, no anger in once more 'losing' their day long argument. "But I fear I cannot go much further without some rest or food I am not half Frost Giant like you."

This made Ragnar laugh and he clapped his friend on the shoulder. "Then I shall have to carry you soon, eh, little one?"

As it turned out before the hour was out, and with no renewed attacks, the two men found just the site they were looking for. It was at the top of a hill, a rock outcropping that resembled the head of a raven. It was a fact that Bjorn noted with a grin of satisfaction. "It is a good omen!"

Ragnar just grunted in the affirmative.

The spot they'd arrived at was in the shadow of a mountain, a narrow defile between two boulders that had been thrown up ages ago by some glacier. The jumbled stones formed a natural cave. It was not deep, but the opening almost allowed Ragnar to stand upright in it.

There was even a pool of rainwater in a rock depression nearby where the two warriors could slack their thirst.

"This tastes sweeter than a maid's kisses." Bjorn laughed as he splashed water on his face between deep gulps.

"I'd still trade it for a horn of mead," Ragnar said. He drank deeply but kept his eyes on the trail behind them.

"Aye, there is that."

The two men pushed themselves to bury the cases of gold and jewels at the back of the cave before taking any real rest. Ragnar used his axe to loosen the dirt then the two of them scooped out the earth using their *spanghelms,* before placing the treasure securely in the holes. Afterward they covered the booty to conceal their work.

The two men tramped down the earth to completely obscure any sign of their digging. When they were finished and stood back, they were satisfied that the ground looked much as it had before they buried the treasure, with no trace of their activity.

Once the loot was safely hidden, the two men collapsed at the mouth of the cave, the last reserves of their prodigious strength of will spent. There the two men slept the clock around and well into the next evening when a sudden rain shower soaked them.

Mani, God of the moon was riding his chariot across the sky when they woke, casting a ghostly light across the rocky terrain that was almost as bright as the winter sun.

Ragnar looked out at the bleak scene and felt a sudden pang of homesickness for the rocky fjords of his homeland. It had been a full two years since he had seen his farmstead and family. He had two fine sons, Sven and Snori, both growing like weeds when last he saw them and by now were almost men who, he was sure, would soon go Viking with him.

It was his wife, Signe, however he missed most. Her courage and wisdom, her smile, and her warmth. It was the thought of providing for her that had driven him on this long trip and that image of her waiting on the farmstead that sustained him through all the perils of the journey.

Her golden hair and her blue, beckoning eyes were suddenly bright in his mind as the stars against the night sky. The almost painful yearning for her ran through him, a shiver that was not born of the cold night air.

He was not one given to long inward journeys but now he thought of his Wyrd, the thread that Uror had woven for him. It was the fate that had been set for him. It was the path he must tread that the three Norns had woven for him, for he could choose to step aside or turn from his fate or to embrace the adversity and plunge headlong into the adventure that was life. He had chosen that destiny, but still, he yearned for Signe's gentle touch.

Soon, he told himself, *soon I will hold you again, my shield maiden-wife and we will laugh and sing once more.*

He had to force her image away from his mind, compelling himself to rise and stretch to shake off his body's ache.

"What is it?" Bjorn asked, startled awake by his sword brother's movement.

"I just needed to rise and move," Ragnar said as he walked around in the small space. "We've had enough rest; let us start back for the longship, I would we were off this accursed land and out to sea. I think maybe you were right, perhaps the little men have given up on us." He took up his great axe, named Limbcutter and swung it above his head for work the stiffness out of his bulked muscles.

The naturalness of the weapon in his hand, the ease of its arcing through the air was a comfort to the warrior. It was an extension of him, a part that called for use even as his cramped legs wanted to walk or his lungs to breathe. It had saved his life and taken many other lives in it use as it sang a song of carnage that he hoped one day would be his herald to Valhalla.

"Now you are talking sense," Bjorn agreed. The smaller man shook himself awake and also stretched. "Let us drink our fill from the fresh water then head out, perhaps we can slip past these brown trolls before sunrise now that we can move swiftly without the treasure."

The two friends drank till their stomachs could hold no more and then Ragnar studied the night sky with a mariner's eye.

"The ocean-sea is beyond that peak," he said pointing to the distant black shape of a mountain outlined against the starry darkness. "We will make for it, and we should cross the river where the ship is hidden in no more than a day or so. Without that Varrangian loot we will fly like Valkeryies!"

The two men laughed and then started off with light hearts and good humor.

And why not?

As sad as they could be for their brothers that had fallen to the painted Skraelings, the two warriors felt joy that those same brothers were already drinking in the hall of the Gods, Valhalla.

Life to the Northmen, Dane, Swede or Rus, was precious; they would fight to preserve it till the last breath. They reveled with all the joys of existence, in bringing new life into the world with children or raising the crops of their farmsteads, but death held no terror to them.

Like the seasons, death itself was part of the cycle of life. Hulda, Goddess of Death had a beauty to her that, while as cold as the ice fields of their homeland was also as familiar.

All men knew death would come. The only shame when it did was to die abed, from old age and the enfeeblement that comes with it. A man's greatest wish was to die well with steel in their hands. That weapon forged from steel would be their key to the door of the great feasting hall of the dead. Each day in the afterlife they would fight eternal battles and each night of that afterlife they would be revived to feast and fete, drinking mead with gods and heroes. Such a death, on the field of battle would draw the eye of Odin's Choosers of the Slain, the Shield Maidens called the Valkyeries

Ragnar and Bjorn had not gone ten minutes down the rocky path into the woods before they became aware of movements in the shadows around them.

"Ragnar—" Bjorn whispered.

"I see," the tall redhead said. "Looks like we get to work off our stiffness sooner than we thought, my brother! It seems their short legs have finally caught up with us."

Just as he spoke the night exploded with peals of thunder, a flash of lightning and the rain became a full-fledged storm. At that moment, rivaling that thunder were the cries of little painted men who swarmed at them. Dozens of the almost naked warriors charged out of the night at the two Northmen while uttering savage, animalistic war yells.

Ragnar and Bjorn exchanged feral grins then yelled their war cry and prayer, "Odin!" as they ran directly at the approaching Skraelings.

Under Mani's bright light and with the driving rain, the two groups of warriors met on a wide spot in the trail. It was a dance of death, a macabre ballet of blood and slaughter that was also a prayer to their various warrior gods. Waves of brown warriors threw themselves at the two invaders with no regard to their own lives, with neither fear nor hesitation at the cost of the combat.

The steel blades, the chainmail and the iron thews of the Northmen were only temporary proof against the superior numbers and the inferior weapons of the brown men. The stone arrows and clubs of the Skraelings were all but useless against the Northmen's hauberks and mail, glancing off or outright breaking on the armor or *spanhelms* but by attrition and sheer numbers the two mighty seafarers were cut and battered on arms, legs and cheeks.

With each and every swing of Ragnar's axe or Bjorn's sword another scrawny brown form fell in a spray of blood and brains, only to be replaced by two more fierce native warriors.

Still, the two friends laughed with savage joy as they slayed. Relishing and embracing the slaughter as others might the caresses of a beautiful woman, the Northmen pressed on. Limbs were hacked, skulls split, and guts spilled in a cascade of death, blossoms of red to present to Hulda as bouquets to a maid.

"The shield maidens will have their pick of this charnel field," Ragnar observed with a lusty shout. "These painted trolls know no fear."

"Nor caution," Bjorn observed as he slashed another warrior down. "You think they would learn their lesson."

The Skraelings indeed did not learn their lesson and continued to swarm at the two invaders with seemingly inexhaustible numbers. The natives even climbed over the bodies of their fellows with wild abandonment with their eagerness to fall on the Northmen. They fought with suicidal fury that even surpassed the two friends.

The clearing where the two seafarers made their stand was a circle of bloody corpses, the ground slippery with gore, and it was that which caused Bjorn to go down to a slick spot as three of the enemy slammed into him.

"I'll see you in Valhalla!" Bjorn managed to scream just as a little warrior brought a rock warclub down to smash his skull to a crimson pulp.

Ragnar gave a cry of anguish and yelled, "We will drink tonight with Thor!" expecting the same fate as his friend, yet the dozen warriors who overwhelmed and held him fast made no move to kill him.

Instead, the Skraelings bound him with stout leather cords and levered him up to a tree to lash him to it.

"Kill me outright, you Nibelungen!" He shouted at them in challenge, "You will get no pleasure in torturing Raganar Longaxe; I will not scream like a woman!"

He cursed himself for being taken rather than outright killed, for now he would not die with a weapon in his hand. He hoped that the Valkyeries would not quibble at the exact cause when his heart beat its last under the hands of the feathered foes.

The brown men chanted in their guttural tongue as they lashed him to an upright dead tree that had been split and burnt at some time in the past by lightning. He tested his bonds, but they knew their knots and he was stuck fast like a bait animal staked out for some predator.

After a time, the Skraelings stood back from the giant Northman and turned to look into the woods as they all seemed to be waiting for something or someone.

"Kill me as a warrior. Give me my axe," Ragnar raged, his own voice competing with the thunder of the storm. "I will not be made sport for..." The words froze in his throat as a hideous figure came shambling up the ravine toward the group.

It was one of the Skraeling race, but so ancient and withered he seemed a shadow of humanity. The wild figure was bedecked with feathers and had a necklace of seashells and finger bones.

Despite his wizened appearance there was an energy in the eyes of the old man such as Ragnar had never seen. The little man began to chant in a strong voice that cut through the cacophony of the storm. He pointed an antler tipped walking stick at the Northman and began an invocation.

Ragnar strained against his bounds and roared his full fury till his throat bled and his hands turned blue against the rawhide bonds. Then the sky flashed white and split once more with such violence that the ground around them shook.

He knew now that if he were to triumph, he would have to look beyond himself for victory. He looked up into the sky and screamed, "Odin, give me strength!"

Suddenly the leather restraints holding him parted and the Northman exploded forward to scoop up one of the painted men as if he were a rag doll, swinging him like a club to lay into the Skraelings with all the rage and hope he could summon.

The brown men came with unbridled fury and untold numbers. They piled on Ragnar, so many that the weight of them immobilized him, wrapping themselves around his chain shirt and legs as well as pinning his arms.

While the Northman raged impotently, barely able to flex his immobilized limbs, the old shaman walked up and touched the antler that topped his walking stick to the center of Ragnar's chest.

A strange blue light, like a lightning born of hell, lept from the antler to dance the brilliant light along the surface of the metal chainmail. The Skraelings holding him shuddered as they felt the strange power of the light but held tight to the Northman who could still could not move, his limbs tingling with a million bee stings of agony.

He felt a chill, deeper than the grave begin to crawl over him from the old man's touch. It was a cold he knew was from the natives magicks of the brown race. While Ragnar feared no man, for he knew his Wyrd was set, the darkness of sorcerers he knew could change that path or end it too soon. It was a menace from the realms beyond that could bend, twist or bend his destiny out of its shape.

"Your sorcery means nothing to me," Ragnar cried, to convince himself more than his enemies. Then he spit directly at the old man and cried, "Thunderer, hear my call, deliver me!"

It is my Wyrd to live and fight and return to my Signe.

When the Northman looked up the old Skraeling shakily walked toward Ragnar. The old man raised his antler raised and pointed it at the stunned intruder.

"I will snap your scrawny throat like a twig," Ragnar laughed impotently. He tried to reach forward for the little man but the brown holding his body would not let him move.

The natives the stared in wonder at the tableau before them of their leader facing the metal clad warrior.

The little holy man walked directly to the giant, dwarfed by Ragnar, yet not cowed. The skraeling muttered again as his followers began to slowly crowd around the statue still figure of Ragnar. The brown men stepped away from the tall Northman and all kept their gaze on their wizened leader, their pained faces grim but their eyes shining with religious fervor. He was unable to move, stunned that he could not.

The little man raised his hands in supplication to the firmament and there was another peel of thunder in the clear sky.

Even Thor has forsaken me in this wilderness, Ragnar thought. *Their skygods are stronger here.*

At the words from the shaman a dancing bolt of green fire crawled from the heavens, moving, it seemed, in slow motion to envelope the transfixed Northman. It was like a great, cosmic hand holding him in place and he was unable to move at all.

Odin take me! Ragnar cried in his mind, but the fire that wrapped him did not burn him, instead, his skin, all a tingle, he felt a great darkness wash over him, but somehow, he knew it was not death, he knew he would not make the journey to the feast hall that day. Perhaps he never would.

And then, all was dark, and Ragnar Longaxe knew no more…

CHAPTER ONE

1766 AD

THE LOST NOT FOUND

"They—they killed them all, Master Blayde!" Stephan Wayne said to his lone companion. There was a quiver of terror in his voice. The fair-haired man was not dressed for forest travel even though he and his companion were in the deep woods of Ohio on a rugged path. His tailcoat was blue wool with gold facings and showed the wear of the journey. He removed his tri-corn hat in a gesture of reverence and in doing so disarrayed his brown hair from the ribbon holding it at his neck. "They killed even the women!"

In front of the two men were a pair of wagons and their contents strewn across the road with the bodies of all those who had been on them dead and bloodied, a scene of slaughter.

"A true fact," the dark-haired companion of the townsman said with a flat tone, his grey eyes hard as flint. "The killers were not interested in slaves or ransom. This is murder for its own sake." He was a tall man with broad shoulders, dressed in green buckskins and obviously comfortable in the wilds.

"But, but the sheer savagery of it, Master Blayde."

"Declinn, please," the woodsman said absent mindedly as he surveyed the forest on either side of the path, "Master Blayde is my Da." When he saw that his tame attempt at levity failed, the taller man added, "It ain't more savage than what the French done in the war; was them that started paying for English scalps." His own long black hair, held back with a rawhide thong, ran nearly to his waist. He carried his long rifle in the crook of his left arm with the gentle caress of a lover as he knelt on the side of the trail examining the traces on the ground around the slaughtered settlers.

"What should we do?" Wayne asked. He was working to compose himself since they had rounded the trail to discover the overturned wagons that had partially blocked the narrow road. There were six settlers, two of them women, scattered where they had died, hacked almost beyond recognition as human beings. It was a level of violence the town-raised man had never seen.

"We move on to Miller's Inn like we intended." Blayde spoke in a quiet voice as he stood.

"We have to at least bury them, sir."

The frontiersman moved to where the oxen had been slain as well, his eyes studying the ground for the full story of what had happened. He spoke without looking up. "That would be the Christian thing, Mister Wayne, the civilized thing to do: but I don't think we have time for that much civilization."

"No time?" Wayne stood uncomfortably at the edge of the path fighting the urge to throw up at the fresh smell of death, averting his eyes from the carnage of the bodies. However even when he looked away to the 'clean' greenery of the forest to try to banish the images he was unsuccessful. He was pale skinned normally but had blanched whiter with the scene before him.

"What in the name of heaven does time have to do with it? We have to be more than the red savages who did this."

"These settler folks were heading to the Miller's place, same as us," Blayde said. "And from the looks of these footprints so are the devils that did this."

"Heading to Miller's?" Wayne repeated. "My god, man, you mean the animals that did this are going toward where my fiancée is?" His facial expression strained to express the feeling of revulsion at this new development and found only a deeper terror.

"Looks to me like it," Blayde said. He stood to his full height and stretched like a great cat. "They came on these folks from ambush on that hill, killed the oxen right off to stop the wagon then rushed the folks on them."

"But how can you know they will go to where Caroline, uh, Miss Miller, my fiancée is…"

"The killers didn't go back down the trail or elst' we'd a run into them. And I suspect with all they took from these poor folks they couldn't head cross country for the dense foliage. I see no horse tracks, so they made packs of the loot to carry their booty: a bunch of killers seems to me."

"We have to catch them then, stop them!" Wayne dcelared. He picked his own traveling pack and the brown Bess musket he had inherited from his brother. He had set it aside when they had come upon the massacre. He started to head up the path, with purpose, but the tall woodsman stopped him.

"Like I said, near as I can figure there are three or four or so, Mister Wayne. They got all these folks had that was worth taking, so they will be moving slow under that burden. If we rush off half-cocked, we're liable to run right into them. That likely as not won't be a cordial meetin'."

"We have to stop them." Wayne brandished his weapon as if it was Excalibur itself. "We can take them from ambush from behind."

"Really? How fast can you load and fire that military musket?"

The brown-haired townsman stared at him trying to reason why such a question was being asked. "Well, I…"

"I can do three shots in a minute if'in I've a powerful reason," Blayde continued. "I'm a might faster with a bow. I guarantee those ahead of us are 'bout as good as I am. I fer one don't want to come on them unexpected like. Fact being, I'd just as soon not come on them at all."

The tall man moved the overturned wagon and adjusted the leather bag slung over his shoulder. He reached into the bag to produce a small but intricately carved wooden crucifix he'd made himself. He set it on the hub of the upper wheel.

"We can't do no more here that this now," Blayde said in a reverent tone. "These good folk won't mind none if we don't plant them till tomorrow or so. We gotta try and get ahead of the bushwackers and see if we can do some good for the living up at the Miller's place. Aside from warning them, we might be able to hold off the bunch that did this from a secure space like the Inn."

Before Wayne could respond, Blayde set of at a gentle trot up the trail and the townsman was forced to follow.

Blayde set a steady trot but seemed in no great haste. The tall frontiersman seemed indefatigable as he set the pace, never breathing hard nor breaking stride, yet he always seemed to know when his shorter companion was at his limits.

Blayde would say he had to examine the rutted trail at these moments, allowing Wayne to collapse on a log or rock to catch his breath and gulp some water without shame.

"We're 'bout an hour or two from catching up to them," Blayde announced. "From here we need to be a little more cautious." He refused a sip of water, instead picking up a smooth pebble to suck on in an almost absent-minded gesture.

Though he appeared to be completely at ease while he rested, his eyes constantly scanned the trail before them.

"You said we shouldn't fight them." Wayne was winded but did his best to not show it.

"Not face on," Blayde said. "But a ways up the trail makes a wide loop around some bottom land, mostly bog. It occurs to me we can cut cross country there and get ahead of them before we rejoin the path."

"But there are so many," Wayne protested. "You said we..."

"We ain't gonna do nothin'," Blayde said rising to his feet. "I'll see if I slow'em down injun style while you run ahead to warn Miller and the others to be ready for their visit."

"See here," Wayne said. "I won't leave you alone to face those blackguards and be slaughtered."

Blayde barely suppressed a gentle grin. "I 'preciate the thought, but I don't plan ta be no sacrificial lamb. I'll slow'em down then skedaddle to join you, once Miller's been warned and either fort up or taken off themselves into the woods to hide."

They were moving at a slower pace then before with the forest road leveling out. It allowed Wayne more breath and time to think and to speak.

"I protested Caroline coming into this god forsaken wilderness." The townsman said with disgust. "I'm from Boston, as she is as well, you know. And she is a refined girl, too refined for this sort of barbarian life; no offense meant."

"None taken," Blayde said laconically.

"In any case, it was her brother's idea to start this trading post and inn two years ago. He wanted 'new opportunities'—he said—All fine and good, but I envisioned a life for us in some mercantile enterprise in Philadelphia if she wanted to have adventure. Yet she felt she needed to come out here to help her

"We have to be more than the red savages who did this."

brother in…"

Blayde held up a hand to silence Wayne then pointed ahead.

"Close," the woodsman whispered. "Sound travels out here so best not to speak much." He motioned for the two of them to slow to a walk.

"The savages are ahead?"

"They may be less than an hour ahead; moving slower than I thought, like they got nowhere special to be. May be some townsmen among them."

"By the Deity, man," Wayne gasped. "You mean white men did that—that horror to those settlers?"

"I've seen all sorts of horror," the woodsman testified. "And believe me, white horror and red horror are all colored the same black of color of gore."

"But white men?"

"You gotta toughin', Master Wayne. There's a good chance to get ahead of them. Question is, why they are out this way at all."

"To meet someone, perhaps?"

"Could be a reason. Or they be getting away from something back the way we came."

"Besides that horror back there?"

"Most sure it's just possible. Back in Kingsburgh where you hired me to guide you, I heard tell that some fellas killed some redcoats over at Fort Ward and took off with a payroll. It is a good bet they might have headed out this way. Could have decided to go to either Fort Pitt or maybe head up toward French country to the northwest. This kind of thing could maybe be them." He shrugged, "But speculation is eating the egg a'fore you crack it. Let's keep moving."

CHAPTER TWO

VISITORS UNWANTED

"Ain't you a pretty little thing," The massive Bull Walker said to the young Seneca girl who brought him a tankard of ale. She also set down a joint of mutton on the table before him. They were in the common room of Miller's Inn on the high road to Fort Pitt, a warm, inviting space with a roaring fire going in the big stone hearth. "I don't remember you here last time I was through here."

"I'd uh sure remember her," Drit Struthers said. He was smaller than his companion with rat-like features and a mouthful of food that he spit pieces of all over himself as he spoke. "She's got a nice set of—"

"Sirah!" A honey-blonde girl in a serving apron and a wimple, chided the men as she poked the fire in the big hearth. She was a few years older than the native girl with wide shoulders and long limbs but with delicate features. "Have you no decency?"

The two leather and fur clad men laughed. There was only one other customer at the inn, a young, redhaired farmer on a journey from the fort after delivering a crop. He sat apprehensively at the far corner of the room his eyes suspiciously focused on his fellow diners.

"Ain't had none of that decency since I weaned me'self, missy," Drit said sending more food flying from his mouth. "And I don't remember you here either last season. And you ain't nothin' for a man to forget neither."

The pretty blonde woman looked sharply at the two bearded men and seemed about to respond but then turned to the native girl instead. "I'll serve these-uh- gentlemen, Nanda. You help my brother in the cook house."

The darkhaired teen cast a hooded look at the men then nodded to the older blonde woman. "Yes, Miss Caroline," she said in a soft voice. She paused at the doorway to the kitchen, looking once more at the other girl with concern, then left.

The two trappers roared with laughter at the expression on the face of the Seneca girl as she exited. "We done scared the little injun away," Bull Walker said. He resembled more a bear than a bull with a full black beard, feathers braided into it and long matted hair blended with the buffalo hide coat he wore. In truth he looked and smelled more animal than human. Combined with his bearskin coat he looked like some pagan war god.

"And I ain't even set a hand on her scalp," Drit said. "Nor no other part of her, yet!"

Caroline Miller wriggled her nose half in disgust at the attitude of the men and half at the miasma of odor that emanated from them. She worked to keep her expression neutral as she freshened the tankards of the two men, taking care to avoid stray hands from each. She caught the farmer's eye who was trying not to stare at the scene and cast a pleading look, but he turned away, doing his best to not be involved.

"You figure we got enough lead on Vickers and them others, Drit?"

"Sure enough," Drit Struthers snickered. He patted a saddle bag on the bench between the men as if it were a pet. "Since we was supposed to meet them south of Fort Ward when we split up, it'll take them days to figure we went west instead. By the time they catch on we'll be spending the money in Fort Pitt." He was a startling contrast to his partner with pale freckled skin, shining red hair making him seem almost ghostly. He was skinny where Bull was broad, yet he out-ate his massive companion three to one.

"That is if the 'Coats don't catch and stretch their scrawny necks." The two men laughed. "And we get to enjoy the fruits of our work." He patted the saddle bags again, caressing them, lovingly.

The two men were seated in the center of the room with their chairs so located to keep their eyes on the door to the outside and the other diner.

"Bring another plate of these greens, girl," Drit snapped when Caroline picked up some empty plates. "And two more ales!"

The girl, willowy wiped a stray hair that had escaped her wimple.

"You haven't paid for the four ales, already, sirahs." She stood firm, willing her clear blue eyes to show no softness. "I am afraid I should have to see some coins first. My brother who…"

"Be you Jonathan Miller's sister?" Bull asked. He scrunched up his thick brows and squinted at the girl. "Of course, you be. I see it in yer cheeks and those eyes."

He chuckled, "I seen the same look last time I was through here from him."

"I remember, Bull," Drit added with a snicker, "He weren't too happy at all same as his filly."

The girl seemed to sense the tone of the conversation had darkened and backed toward the crude bar to set the plates and tankards down.

"Jonathan," she called out the open door to the stone cookhouse, "Come in here, please."

Bull and Drit set aside their food and pushed back from the table with synchronized sighs.

"I sore wanted to fill up," Drit said, "a'forn I got all my digestion upset."

The girl looked worried and called again, "Jonathan, I need you. Now!"

There was noise from outside then a tall man with the same wheat colored hair as Caroline came through the doorway. "What is it, sis?" He said impatiently, "I have to finish the pies or…"

Jonathan stopped in his tracks in his tracks when he saw the two men at the table. "You," he snapped, pointing at the men. "I told you two not to ever come back to…"

Suddenly Bear's flintlock erupted in flame and smoke and the lead ball from the pistol slammed Miller back into the log wall of the room.

"Jonathan!" the girl screamed. She ran to her sibling as he slid down the wall where he left a blood smear on it. He was bleeding badly from a wound on the right side of his chest, his pale skin went pasty white his eyes wide with surprise.

"Caroline," the man murmured, his eyes unfocused, "it suddenly got so cold."

The girl grabbed her wimple off and used it in an attempt to staunch the blood from the gunshot wound.

Drit laughed. "Good shot, Bull, but missed him plumb off dead center."

"I must be drunk," his huge partner said, "I was aiming for his head!" This made the skinny man roar with laughter and Bull soon joined him in cackling.

"You filthy animals!" the girl screamed.

The lone farmer jumped up from his seat, the violence finally too much for him. He grabbed up a dinner knife and started to move toward them, but Drit, almost without effort or sighting, snapped his wrist and sent a tomahawk whirling across the room.

The hatchet stuck the innocent guest in the forehead with such force that it sent him arching backward to slam over the tabletop and drop to the floor very dead.

Caroline screamed again and launched herself at Bull, hands held before her like claws.

Bull easily avoided her attack, pinned the girl's arms to her and swept her off her feet in a tight bear hug. This only set the girl to screaming louder and the men to a new round of raucous laughter.

"She got spunk, Bull," the thin thug snickered. "Think you can hold her, or do you need some help?" He moved behind the bar and began searching for anything that he could appropriate.

"Day I need your help with a female will be day after Judgment Day, boy!" Just as he spoke, the Seneca girl, Nanda came charging through the door with a kitchen knife raised to strike.

Bull tossed Caroline aside as if she were so much baggage and spun to face the new threat.

The tiny native teen might as well have been attacking a buffalo for the ease with which Bull evaded her attack. Then he back-handed her across the face. The blow sent her sprawling over a table which she then rolled off of to lie dazed, on the floor.

"I see what yah mean, Bull," Drit said. "You got a real special way with women."

The massive Walker moved with a grace that belied his size and grabbed the hair of the semi-conscious native girl lifting her head.

"You want this scalp, Drit?" He laughed as he shook the teen like a rag doll. "Be a fine souvenir for if we ever run into the boys again."

"No!" Caroline screamed. She was leaning on the table, winded from Bull's rough handling, but found strength to gasp, "Have you no decency at all?"

Bull pulled Nanda almost to her knees by her hair where she dangled limp. He pulled a long knife and brandished it before her unfocused eyes. "I got all the decency I need, blondie." He cast a glance at the gasping Jonathan Miller. "That dog spawn of a brother of yours accused me o'cheatin' him on some furs last season back."

"Well, you were," Drit pointed out.

"Ain't the point," Bull snarled. "Me made sport o' me in front of folks and chased me from the trading post with a long rifle." He started to touch the knife to Nanda's forehead but stopped, distracted by a glint of yellow that spilled out at the neck of her buckskin dress. "What's this?"

He caught up the revealed medallion on the blade of his knife to study it. It was tiny, beautifully carved figure of a helmeted and bearded man with two ravens on his shoulders.

"This is pure gold!" Bull gasped. He sheathed his knife and yanked the medallion from the rawhide thong around her neck.

"That is mine!" Nanda now shocked awake protested. "It is sacred!"

"It's mine now," Bull dropped the girl to the floor and examined the medallion. "This ain't no trade good; it looks real old and real expensive like."

"Sacred," the Seneca repeated.

"Where'd you get it girl?"

The native glared at him with feral intensity so that he backhanded her again. "I asked you a question, girl."

Her answering stare was full of cold hate.

"Stop this," Caroline called. She was obviously torn between going to her fallen brother and aiding the younger girl.

"Ain't gonna get no injun to talk that way, Bull," Drit hopped over the bar and went straight to the blonde girl. He grabbed her arm and twisted until she cried out in pain.

"You talk, injun," Drit said calmly, "or I break her arm clean off." To emphasize his point he twisted so Caroline sobbed in agony.

"Sacred," Nanda repeated with a look of defeat in her dark eyes. "But I tell; no hurt Miss Caroline." The two thugs stared at her in challenge until she continued, "It belongs to Far Away Warrior, legend of my people."

Bull almost dropped the medallion and Drit did drop Caroline when they heard the name.

"Drit, my brother," Bull said, "Even I heard of that injun legend."

"Yes, sir," Drit grinned. "I think we just made the find of a lifetime!"

+++

The darkness swirled before The Sleeper, the echoes of screams and the clash of blades in the distance. There was no pain, no pleasure in the void. For a long time there had been no awareness, but now The Sleeper felt his separate limbs and his body felt chilled and hot at the same time. And The Sleeper heard the horn call in the distance, and he was ready.

CHAPTER THREE

MORE TROUBLE

Declinn Blayde led the town-bred Wayne off the track and into the deeper woods. Their progress was laborious, but the frontiersman would not slacken the pace. "No point in us running if we come into the tail end of that slaughter pack," Blayde said. "We gotta push ahead of them, this is the only way."

"I'm not complaining, Master Blayde, but If I constrain your progress, please feel no guilt in leaving me to press ahead; Miss Miller's safety is by far a greater import. You must reach her and her brother to warn them."

The woodsman stopped for just a moment to look back at the clearly exhausted Wayne with a slight grin. "Well said, sir, but fear not—you're doing fine. I can't run you into the ground, else you'll be in no shape to fight for your lady when we get there."

The two men rested infrequently but moved steadily through the swampy land that cut across the countryside intent on bisecting the long loop of the path the bandits had taken.

It was almost nightfall when the two emerged onto the wagon road on the other side of the lowlands.

"Have we beaten them?" Wayne asked when the two paused at the edge of the wilderness track.

The woodsman knelt to examine the ground, studying it for signs of any recent passage. "No one's been along this but some deer for a good bit." He looked up and smiled. "We're way ahead of them, I reckon."

"Then we shall lay a trap for them here?"

"I've been thinking on that; I figure we'd be better served to hightail it to the Miller place and prepare the folks. If there are enough bodies there, we fort up, if not, hide them in the woods and then take on these fellas ourselves."

"You know best, Master Blayde."

"It'll mean pushing even harder, and in the dark. At least it will be a full moon, so this road will be well lit enough if we're careful."

The city bred man, his clothes showing the tatters and dirt of their flight, took a deep breath. He looked down the trail back toward where the ravagers would come and nodded. "What needs to be done, sir, I shall do. Lead on!"

"Good lad." The scout rose and, without another word, took off at a light trot. Wayne reshouldered his musket and followed as best he could.

+++

"I want sass talk from you, missy," Bull Walker said as he backhanded Nanda hard enough to drive the Indian to her knees. "Ah'll ask you fer an opinion." The massive man and the native were standing in front of the three pack animals had been loaded with the spoils that the two men had gathered from the inn.

"Don't put'er down all the way, Bull," Drit said with a hoarse laugh. "I don't wanna have to carry the trash."

Caroline Miller, though her hands were bound, quickly stepped between the blustering giant and the Seneca.

"Let her be," the blonde said. Her hair was in disarray and a bruise reddening on her left cheek, but her eyes still showed defiance. "You've no reason to manhandle her."

"And you back talkin' me, drudge?" Bull raised his and to strike her, but his compatriot's voice halted him.

"Easy, Bull." Drit cautioned, "She won't be worth spit in trade if you damage her face anymore."

The two bandits had piled their pack horses and the two prisoners had been expecting to be murdered—or worse—but to their surprise had been forced to accompany the killers who had stopped on the ridge overlooking the trading post when one of the packs began to slip off a horse.

"Good in trade?" Caroline gasped.

"Still don't like a sassy female," Bull said in a subdued tone. He fixed the kneeling girl with a cold stare. "This one though has no trade value with the Chickasaw." He leaned in, "Now know this, girl; you take us to where you got this trinket and we'll let you go, but you do us wrong and I swear by Moses' staff I'll make you regret being born."

Nanda returned Bull's stare, a trickle of blood at the corner of her mouth. Her dark eyes blazed with a black fire of hate.

"She don't care on herself, Bull," the pale companion said, "But she I reckon won't take it well if'n we slice a toe or finger off of this here high class filly." He pulled a ten-inch blade, stepped over to point it at Caroline. "And that won't hurt her resale all that much." He smiled and then chuckled.

"What?' Caroline gasped again, "You swine!" She slapped the blade aside and moved to scratch at Drit's eye, but Bull reached out huge hand and grabbed the delicate girl by her hair. He all but lifted her from the ground and caused her to cry out in pain.

"You shut up," he said flatly. "And behave like a lady or you'll be a nine-toed one."

He laughed at his own joke.

"You can't just leave Jonathan and that other man in there," Caroline said. "Not without a decent Christian burial." She had watched her brother breathe his last less than an hour before but had internalized her grief for the sake of survival.

"You don't tell us what we can do," Bull hissed. "And you just thank your god you ain't with'em. Now just shut up while re-secure these packs."

The blonde woman, crouched by the native, whose hands were also tied and used her sleeve to staunch the blood on the girl's lip.

"Do not worry, Miss Caroline," the girl said quietly. She winced at the blonde's touch. "I only worry that they will hurt you."

"Never mind me. After they killed Jonathan, I knew there was no human hope—I have prayed for divine aid."

"May your god protect you," the native said. "As I know my gods will punish these men for the desecration they plan."

"What do you mean?"

"The necklace he took from me," the girl whispered. "It is from the Far Away Warrior."

"Who is that?"

"Long ago a man came from across the sea, a great warrior. And with him he brought a great treasure. He killed many of my people, but our gods were stronger than his and he was vanquished. But the place of his downfall where he and the treasure were buried was made sacred for the bloodshed."

"And you know where this is?"

The native simply nodded.

"You don't have to tell them," Caroline said. "They will only use that treasure to no good."

"To keep them from hurting you. You and Mister Jonathan were good to me and my people. When last winter there was much hunger, he gave much to my tribe. And medicine when there was sickness. I must do this."

"No," the blonde insisted. "They cannot profit from their horror, I will endure whatever I must."

"It will be well," Nanda said, giving a shy smile. "I have faith in my gods as you do in yours. There will be justice."

Just then Bull called. "On your feet, you two baggage, you're gonna lead us to where you got that dohicky, chicken. And do it as easy as you please, and that's a fact."

+++

The calling was insistent, the howl of Fenris, the great wolf and the distant war drums growing louder. The beat of wings and the caws of Memory and Thought spoke the message, "Soon, warrior. Soon, Limbcutter will drink again."

CHAPTER FOUR

ARRIVAL

"Is there no end to the terror of this horrible wilderness?" Stephen Wayne said, turning away from the smell of death that greeted him and Declinn Blayde when they opened the door to Miller's Inn.

The two men had arrived at the trading post an hour after sunup to find the bodies of Jonathan Miller and the farmer still laying where they had been callously murdered. It was clear the trading post had been ransacked as well.

"You said that the killers of the caravan were behind us," Wayne said when he had regained his composure.

"This wasn't that bunch," Blayde said. He walked around the whole perimeter of the building, inside and out with a tracker's eye, noting the plates eaten off of, the tankards that had been used and the signs of struggle both inside and outside the building. "This was only two, maybe three men. Came on two horses, left with three, heavy laden."

"Not the same bunch? There are more monsters in this hellish forest?" Wayne's voice was shrill as he frantically ran through all the rooms and to the outbuildings searching for his fiancée and yelling, "Caroline!"

"Save your breath, Master Wayne," Declinn called from the edge of the clearing. "There are two women that went with whoever was here."

"Caroline?"

"One was a white woman by her perfume, one was wearing moccasins."

"We must be after them then," Wayne, despite the exhaustion from the night's run his eyes were wide, and he was enervated.

"We will," Blayde said. "But we get some food first and you get ten minutes rest."

"But—"

"No buts—This is gonna be harder run than we had last night. We have to catch them unawares to make sure the women folk are safe."

Despite his desire to race off immediately as soon as Wayne sat down to eat the pace of the last night's excursion took over, he fell into an exhausted sleep. Declinn let the man rest, gathering a small bag of food and found a second powder horn to add to his own.

The woodsman let himself rest by the townsman, knowing he would need his full reserves for what was to come. He allowed himself to doze for almost an hour then and, as was his want, woke fully refreshed and alert. Only then did he wake the exhausted Wayne.

"What—why did you let me sleep?"

"You're gonna need the rest. From here we don't stop. Our only break is that the women are on foot—I suspect whoever did that inside has the animals too loaded with loot."

Wayne shook himself, splashed water in his face and snarled, "You always say that— about not stopping."

"It's true enough this time as well. We still have to get the lady, but now we have to get her away from those that have her before whoever is following catches up."

Wayne blanched and looked stunned.

"Definition of between a rock and hard place, I'd say," Blayde noted grimly. "Well, let's get movin'."

Without another word the woodsman took off without waiting for his companion who had no choice but to follow.

+++

"You slow us down anymore, baggage," Bull Walker snarled at Caroline Miller, "and trade value or no, I'll hurt you good."

They were cutting trail through rough country at the direction of Nanda, heading toward the sacred ground of her people. The rocky terrain was hampering the progress with the horses shying so frequently that they had decided to cache the loot from Miller's so the animals had room for any of the treasure yet to be found. Now the light was the orange glow of a setting sun and they had to move all the more carefully for the long shadows. This caused the horses to move slowly, picking their way carefully among the loose gravel on the slopes of the hilly trail.

"Ain't her that's the problem, Bull," Drit said. "This red drudge is leading us all catiwompus in these hills." He yanked the rope he had tied around Nanda's neck causing the teen to stumble.

"No, I lead true," she said. "This way to place of the Far Away Warrior. Not many steps now."

Bull yanked on Caroline's lead rope with an angry tug. "Well, she's been dragging her feet."

"I have not," the blonde protested. "I twisted my ankle a while ago, I can't go any faster."

"Not far," Nanda insisted, "Just over the hill, I tell the truth."

The two kidnappers both gave wide, smiles and pulled harder on the restraining ropes around the women's necks. "Then, let's move on," Bull roared. "And don't you slow us anymore, drudge."

He pulled on Caroline which forced the woman to limp along as the four of them led the horses up to the crest of the hill where they all paused.

"Glory be," Drit muttered, "The red baggage weren't lyin!"

Ahead of them in a shallow valley were more rolling hills but these covered with old growth vegetation. It was a rock outcropping in the center of the valley that drew their attention. The natural, shallow cave that cut through the granite had been decorated with native pictographs and had flowers and small offerings of food set before the mouth of the cave.

"Let's not hurt these horses on the way down," Bull said, the blonde prisoner forgotten for the moment. He started to lead the mount forward then paused to look back. "You follow on with us, woman—you try to run, and I don't care to trade you nowhere."

"I will help you, Miss Caroline," the native said. She moved to stand by the blonde and helped support her as they rested for a moment against a house sized boulder before they began to make their way down the decline.

The two kidnappers, meanwhile, led the horses down the slope and into the brush cover of the valley floor. The men only cast an occasional glance back toward the women, their eyes focused mostly on the pagan shrine before them.

"We got it made, Bull. With the payroll and the gold from this, we don't even have to go back for the stuff from Miller's."

"Could be. If it is we just lit out straight for French country, we'll get more trade value on the pound notes there." He was breathing hard but not from exertion. "That is if there is anywhere near the gold in that red church as the legends say there is."

"Go, run," Caroline whispered to the native. "Save yourself."

"No. I will not leave you until you can follow."

"Not with this ankle, I can't. Doesn't matter. They will kill you now that they've come here."

The Indian girl, letting the blonde lean most of her weight on her, shook her head. "I believe in the power of my gods, Miss. Hawenniyo, the creator and He-no—who calls the lightning—will protect us."

The two women topped the hill and began to slowly move down the loose rock of the slope, the blonde moving gingerly, favoring her right ankle.

Suddenly a hand shot out from behind the boulder and fastened on Caroline's arm.

+++

The war horns trumpeted, the howls of the berserkers reached a fever pitch and Huggin and Muggin cawed, "prepare, warrior, soon you are called to your duty."

+++

When Bull and Drit reached the bottom of the hill they walked across the depression with fixed expressions of extasy, their movements almost like sleepwalkers. From the valley floor the shrine ahead of them was edged in the golden light of the setting sun and looked truly other worldly.

The natural cave formed by the collision of two large boulders long ago had been enlarged and a wooden frame added before it, on which were pictographs and native ward signs. There was a crudely carved wooden figure standing beside the entrance to the shrine, a rough form of a helmeted and armored man that stood near eight feet tall. It had a long axe in his carved hands. Weather had smoothed the details, but it was clearly not of a native figure, but of a European man with full beard.

The two kidnappers stopped at the outer perimeter of the offerings before the shrine, struck with a rare moment of awe in their life. Close up the wooden image in front of the shrine was also wearing a golden necklace that had been placed on the form. Bull stepped forward and fingered the jewelry with a shaking hand.

"This is it," he murmured. "We are set for life, brother."

The rodent featured Drit stepped past his partner to venture into the dark maw of the cave. He dropped to his knees to open the small oak casket that was resting against the far wall. It was bound with aged brass hinges and bordered by ancient leather pouches, all but rotted through and showing the glint of silver coins. When Drit opened the casket, it was piled high with jewelry, chalices and gold and coins. He laughed and began to sing, "We got it made, we got it made!"

"Wonder why them redskins didn't just grab all this?" Bull asked.

"Who cares, brother, we got it now."

Bull patted the necklace on the statue then dropped beside his friend and joined him in laughing. "We can get the baggage to dig up any more there is for us, brother. We just camp here tonight then load the horses and off we go tomorrow."

"Yeah, why work when they can do it!" He looked back up the hill toward the women. "Hey—look!"

+++

"Soon, soon soon," the siren call of the ravens' echoed. "Limbcutter will drink and horns will sound. Prepare, warrior, prepare!"

CHAPTER FIVE

REUNION

Caroline almost screamed but a second hand over her mouth stopped her. "Easy, Dearheart," Stephen Wayne whispered. "We're here to save you."

Nanda turned with fingers formed into claws until she saw Declinn Blayde beyond the townsman, hidden behind the boulder. "*Haya'daha*!" she gasped, which was Seneca for 'he who makes pictures.'

"We must go quickly," Declinn whispered. "While they are gloating on their success."

They moved back up the slope, but the blonde's ankle could not support her weight.

"Take this," the woodsman handed his long rifle to Nanda then scooped up Caroline into his arms. "Let's get!"

The four moved as quietly as possible back down the side of the slope opposite the Indian shrine, but the loose gravel echoed in the evening air.

+++

"Hey, them women ain't on the hill," Drit said when he looked up at the slope. The escaping women were already over the crest of the hill, their saviors unseen and out of sight.

"Leave'em," Bull moved in close to stare at the golden necklace on the guardian statue, squinting at it in the failing light. The intricate metalwork was scribed with runes and symbols and incrusted with jewels. "A night in the woods shivering will make them baggage pliable. Let's get a fire going and holdup in this cave afore worrying about them. I want to be up early to look for them then to dig out the rest of this treasure for us."

+++

The four fugitives headed away from the shrine with Declinn carrying Caroline and Wayne walking rearguard, glancing back in the event the kidnappers should follow. When they had gone sufficient distance to risk conversation they paused at the top of the rise in the land where they could look back behind them from cover and rest.

"They don't seem to be following us," Wayne cast his glance back while hugging the blonde tight to him.

"May not think it worth chasing the ladies," Blayde accepted his rifle back

A hand shot out from behind the boulder and fastened on Caroline's arm.

from Nanda and took a sip of water.

"They do not think we can survive without them," the Seneca teen said with bitterness. "Always the white think less of women."

"About right," the woodsman agreed. "Seems us white folks undervalue lots of things that matter—not the least of which is you ladies."

"Barbaric," Wayne whispered.

"They are monsters, Stephen," Caroline sobbed into her fiancée's shoulder. She hugged him fiercely. The last hours of constant tension had finally worn through her emotional armor. "They killed Jonathan and that other man with no thought…" She began to cry softly.

"I know, Dearheart," Stephen said. "We followed but had to wait until we could get you alone for your safety."

"We have to go back and give Jonathan a Christian burial," Caroline said when she could control her sobs. "Those beasts didn't—"

"'Fraid we can't do that, ma'am," Blayde said. When she started to protest, he pointed back toward the trading post. It was full night now and there was a distinct glow on the horizon, orange and white against the dark sky with clouds promising a storm to come.

"What is that?" Wayne asked.

"I suspect it's Miller's place burning."

"Burning?"

"Could be that storm but I suspect it is them's what did the two wagons."

"Who?" Caroline asked. The two men explained finding the slaughtered caravan and circumventing the killers.

"Why would they burn the trading post?" Stephen asked.

"Not sure," Blayde said, "except maybe pure anger."

"Anger?"

"Takes a powerful bit of anger to burn a building," the woodsman said, "but I got no idea why."

"What do we do now?" Wayne asked.

"We sure can't go back the way we came," the woodsman said. "If those folks followed the same trail we did, I sure don't want to run into them. We were only a couple hours ahead of them anyway."

"Why would they follow us?" Wayne asked. "Why not proceed to Fort Pitt?"

"I suspect they would head to the fort, most likely," the frontiersman said, "but still not a chance I want to take since we didn't hide our trail. I say we head cross country toward the fort rather than the trail, but it will be tricky with weather coming in."

"We will need supplies," Wayne stated. "The ladies are at the end of their endurance, and I must admit, so am I."

"I will do what must be done," Caroline said. "I will not let my life end here."

"Well said," Blayde agreed.

"The men left many supplies with the cache," Nanda said. "There was food with their stolen things."

"That decides it then," Blayde said. "We can go back as far as to where those two cached things from Millers and strike off for the fort. It a gamble, but a good one."

The four moved back down the trail, this time in the full darkness of a cloudy sky. The moon would not rise for its second night for several hours but the scent of moisture, a storm to come filled the night. Their progress was at a snail's pace for the need for safety. They moved in silence with Blayde leading, followed by Nanda, Caroline and with Wayne bringing up the rear. The group paused every few minutes to listen for any sign they were being followed. There was none.

They stopped again just as the moon topped the horizon to catch their breaths.

"We are not far from the place they left the supplies," Nanda said when the ground leveled out. "At the tree which caught fire from lightning. It is black."

"They all look black in this darkness," Wayne noted.

"I think this is the one," Blayde called back from several feet ahead. "Partially fallen over?"

"That is the one," the native agreed. "They buried the bags and food there." She pointed to a dip in the land where brush had been moved to conceal the shallow hole where the supplies had been buried.

Blayde handed his rifle to Nanda and began to dig, using his tomahawk to loosen the earth above the cache.

Wayne sat with his arm around the exhausted Caroline, who leaned against him enjoying the momentary peace. "I promise to get you out of his wilderness," he whispered, to her. "I should have protected you from this, you should never have let you come out here to face this ugliness."

"No," she said. "Jonathan needed me; it was good until those monsters showed up. He did so much good for so many out here—you can't condemn the frontier—there are many good people here."

"But you—" he began as a peal of thunder ripped the night and an arrow whistled out the darkness and passed through his hat.

Several figures raced out of the night, charging at the four fugitives as rain began to hammer the woods.

Many things happened simultaneously. Nanda raised and fired Blayde's rifle to shoot one attacker dead center, killing him. The woodsman whirled and tossed his tomahawk which struck a second attacker.

Wayne tried to get his musket up to bear but he was hampered by Caroline leaning against his body. When he did, the gun was a flash in the pan and did not fire. The third assailant bowled the townsman over, a knife in his hand. Wayne hit the ground, grabbing the weapon hand of the attacker trying to control the blade. The two rolled on the ground while the startled Caroline yelled in terror.

Blayde drew his own knife and charged a fourth brigand who produced a pistol, but Declinn slammed into him and drove his knife into the bandit's throat. As the two of them fell to the ground the frontiersman wrestled the gun from the now dead attacker, rolled, cocked and fired it. The ball from the pistol hit the man fighting with Wayne, felling him.

Caroline had recovered Wayne's musket by now and waved it at the darkness of the forest, but no more figures came from the night woods.

Blayde recovered his rifle from Nanda and quickly reloaded it, shielding the pan from the drenching rain, prepared for more attacks that did not come. Then he went to each of the four men, finding the last one, the one he had shot, still alive.

"Damn you, Bull," The wounded bandit gasped. He, like the others was a white man, though roughly made and dressed in near rags. He was bleeding badly from a chest wound, his breathing coming in wet gulps. His eyes were wide open, but he was not seeing what was before him, only some memory. "You ain't gonna get away from me…" He took a huge intake of breath, then suddenly coughed once and was dead.

"What just happened?" Wayne asked.

Blayde knelt by the dead man, but his eyes were attempting to peer through the rain back toward the shrine.

"These guys were the ones that took that wagon train," the woodsman surmised.

"And Miller's," Wayne added. "They must have thought we were that Bull fellow and his friend."

"Problem is, we ain't," Declinn said. "But now them back at the shrine know we ain't just the women folk. I suspect they will be comin' this way directly."

CHAPTER SIX

HOLY WAR

Bull Walker came awake slowly, some dream still clinging to his thoughts and for a moment was not sure where he was. Then he looked over at his compatriot snoring beside him, a hand full of gleaming jewels on the sleeping Drit's chest.

Bull grinned. He stepped out of the cave mouth into the chill night air. The moon was up, the damp smell of rain to come making the evening crisp.

The bandit stood by the totem statue in front of the shrine, running a hand over the pitted surface of the wood till his calloused fingers rested on the golden necklace. He smiled and lifted the necklace over the head of the bearded figure and slipped it over his own head.

Then he laughed. "Yeah," he said in a quiet voice. "Got it made this time. Them fools wandering around looking for the payroll we took; now that's pig feed compared to this."

He patted the necklace and strutted around the front of the cave giggling softly to himself. Then he heard almost simultaneously Caroline's scream and a gunshot a distant peal of thunder.

"Drit, up," he yelled as he ran for his rifle. "Trouble!"

+++

"No, I will not wait here or be pushed aside," Caroline insisted. Blayde and Wayne had stripped weapons from the four attackers and Wayne told the women to hide.

"But it will be dangerous, they will know you are not alone and unarmed."

"No point arguing with her," Blayde said. "She's got more spine than most soldiers. She's better to be with us than off on her own in all this."

Nanda held up the rifle she had secured from the bandits. "I will fight." She had used a coat from one of the fallen men to create a shroud to protect her weapon from the rain while she loaded it.

"See, we got them outnumbered now," Blayde noted with a wry grin. "Better we got to them than make them come to us, better to be the hunter."

Caroline brandished the flintlock pistol, now reloaded and half-cocked under her own found coat. "Yes, let us get them."

Wayne looked at the blonde and shrugged. "As you wish, Dearheart. Whatever, we will face all that is to come together."

+++

Bull and Drit moved quickly up the trail, guns primed and ready when the first burst of the rain drenched them.

"How could they get a gun?" Drit asked.

"Maybe got back to the cache. I left some there for later. And I bet they shot at some hoot owl that scared them or just from the thunder. I swear I'll strip the hide from that blonde vixen for bringing me out in this storm."

"Might just as well do them both for good," Drit said. "More trouble than their worth, special now that we got us a king's ransom, we don't need them for trade."

"You got that, your majesty," Bull laughed as he bowed. "We don't need nothin' nor nobody."

+++

The sound of ravens called The Sleeper's name with a song of life and death that he had not heard for a long time.

"Warrior," they said. "You swore on the oath ring to protect the treasure of Sven Bluetooth. Now is the time."

Once more he saw the blue-white arc of the shaman's staff again dance against his eyelids and felt the hot touch of it against his chest.

Visions of the wife, Signe, he'd left behind called to him, or was it a Valkyrie's song that filled his ears?

The sculpture that stood before the cave of the shrine began to change, the worn wood surface to waver and undulate, the texture of it to transmute. The grain of the wood became desiccated flesh, and the sculpted chainmail once more was metal, now rusted and aged.

The Sleeper opened his eyes and Ragnar Longaxe was awake.

The darkness was no longer complete and enveloping, now there was a blue tinted nightscape before him. As rain began to fall, the drops were a hard caress that pinged in steady rhythm off his spanghelm, once more he felt his fingers on the haft of his axe, Limbcutter. They moved with stiffness but his fingers regripped it and he slowly raised the weapon high.

"Odin," he tried to pray, but the sound that came from him was a croaking, rasping thing, a sound torn from a tormented soul. "I rieve for you!"

Ragnar Longaxe moved his booted feet, the steps scattering the offerings that fanned out before the shrine as he marched into the night to fulfill his oath.

+++

Bull Walker charged ahead of his shorter companion, his feet slipping in the muddy terrain, sliding down the far side of the hill. The initial cloudburst was blinding in its intensity but after a few minutes it became a gentler steady downpour.

"Slow down, Bull," Drit called as he followed. "I can't see my own feet in this."

"They big enough should be pretty clear." He spoke as the two moved up the trail by memory, the faint starlight making it a slow process.

"Hey, don't make fun, I had a growth spurt."

"Just don't shoot me by mistake."

"My eyes ain't so bad I can't tell a moose from a miss," Drit snorted at his own joke. Even Bull laughed.

When the two men had reached a wide spot in the trail a voice called from the shelter of the trees,

"Drop your guns and live!" Blayde ordered.

The two kidnappers immediately tried to fire at the sound of his voice was but both rifles misfired in the rain.

The four fugitives returned fire but only Nanda's rifle and Wayne's Brown Bess discharged shot. Both shots missed the two targets.

Blayde discarded his rifle and charged forward, tomahawk and knife in hand.

Bull swung his rifle as a club, but Blayde dodged, and the stock shattered on a tree. When Declinn closed with the huge man he stabbed him, but the knife could not penetrate the buffalo hide coat.

Bull roared and grabbed the woodsman in a bear hug slamming Declinn against a tree so hard he dropped his tomahawk.

Wayne swung his musket at Drit and the rodent faced man parried with his own weapon's barrel.

Nanda charged forward, knife in hand to come to Wayne's aid as a blast of thunder boomed directly over them. A bolt of lightning sliced into a tree to the side of the trail, exploding it into hundreds of fragments. The six people were knocked to the ground by the concussion of the strike and were all showered with slivers of wood.

Then a second lance of celestial light revealed the desiccated figure of Ragnar Longaxe. The armored revenant was a nightmare made real, his eye sockets empty hollows, his cheeks sunken with parchment skin and teeth exposed between skinless lips. His armor was tattered and chinked but the rusty axe he swung still promised destruction with every blow.

Caroline screamed just as another peal of thunder blasted the night and the rain became more torrential.

The Norse apparition forced air though its desiccated lungs in what came out at as a wheezing bark. He began to move forward slowly, the axe held in preparation.

"Gawd of hell!" Bull yelled. He pulled himself to his feet and tried to run but the revenant sliced his axe into the massive man's back, driving the blade deep.

Bull let out a gasped exclamation, his arms flung wide and fell to the ground.

Ragnar yanked the axe from the dead man and turned to face Drit.

The rodent featured man stood terrified, urine running down his leg and made low moaning sounds as the armored apparition moved toward him.

Ragnar raised the axe and brought it down with such force that it split the kidnapper from skull to groin, nearly perfectly in half.

Then the revenant turned toward Caroline. She stood frozen with the horror of what she had seen. She re-cocked the pistol and pulled the trigger, this time the gun fired, and the lead ball slammed into the walking corpse but to no effect.

"Run!" Wayne called to the blonde woman, but she was too paralyzed by the Northman's approach to move.

The townsman raced across the open space toward the woman while at the same time Declinn Blayde barreled into the Northman from the side.

The woodsman was able to turn the undead warrior from the girl, causing the Northman to stumble, but then it brought the haft of the axe down onto Declinn's back. Blayde was driven to his knees and the revenant shoved him away to raise the weapon for a fatal blow.

"*Ehsenihe*," Nanda yelled as she stepped between the warrior and Blayde. "You have to quit this!" Ragnar hesitated, his axe at the top of its arc. "You are confused—*deyodaha*, this man is not evil." When the undead guardian still did not move, she went to the fallen form of Bull and pulled the necklace from his neck, holding it up to the warrior. "This is the one who took your treasure. We return it to you." She stood fearlessly before the Norse giant and offered the necklace up with both hands, bowing her head in supplication. The undead warrior slowly lowered the axe and extended a bony hand to take the jewelry from the native. The Seneca backed away as the warrior looked from the necklace to her. "Nanda!"

Caroline gasped as she ran to embrace the girl.

Ragnar stared at the blonde woman and felt a memory stir within him. He took a single step forward and forced sound out from his tortured lungs to moan, "Signe!"

At that moment the sky erupted again with a blast of thunder and a spear of lightning struck the spanghelm of the warrior.

The heavenly fire raced through the body of the revenant, sparks dancing from the links of the chainmail, and causing the whole of his body to shiver and shake. Smoke issued from his eye sockets and limbs and then the giant collapsed in on himself.

In moments the Northman was a pile of bones and smoking clothing, Limbcutter's haft a burning wick, sputtering in the rain.

EPILOGUE

THE JOURNEY'S END

The four friends stood stunned staring at the smoking corpse that had been the Northman on the ground as it rapidly decomposed before their eyes.

Wayne and Caroline crossed themselves.

"The hand of Providence." Declann said with a quiet voice. "Pure Providence."

"No," Nanda said, kneeling reverently by the smoldering remains of the guardian giant. "He-no, who calls the lightning is protecting us for saving the treasure."

The rain stopped then, as if it had done its work and the gibbous moon escaped the clouds.

"Well," Blayde said, "I reckon we gather up the weapons and take that necklace back to the shrine—and get the horses. I think we want to be long gone by sunup."

The others had no problem agreeing and soon they were on their way.

+++

In the void Ragnar Longaxe smiled. He knew it was the hand of Odin through his lightning spear, Gungnir, that had called him.

He heard the battle song again and felt the wind of the Valkyries wings.

I will see you again, Signe, and will drink with you yet this night, my brother *Bjorn,* Ragnar thought even as the final fingers of the darkness embraced him. *And we will sing of how I kept my oath!*

RAGNAR'S REQUIUM

The cold of sleep
Where his bones did keep
Could not the Northman hold
Though fought in death
Long past the rest
And his burden was awesome to behold
His blade was sharp and he

Felt no fear
As he fought from beyond the veil
To find of heroic kind
And escape the Skraling thrall,
"Lord Odin," he cried as his enemies died,
"Accept me to your side-
Though Hulda turns 'way
On this, my endless day
I long to sup with thee."
And One-Eye spoke
With a thunder stroke
"Your Wyrd is plain to see-
Though you've
Waited long for a
Dying song
You were meant to sit
By me!"

THE END

THE RED SISTERHOOD

PROLOGUE

They saw the smoke from the burning cabins before they saw the cabin itself. It curled up like a lariat through the morning mists of the Appalachian Mountains. Then they smelled the acrid odor of the burning wood and flesh and the horses pulling the supply laden wagon, shied.

"Stay here with the wagon," the darkhaired woman at the reins said to the five-year old who sat beside her. The husky woman climbed down from the wagon seat and handed him the traces.

"What's wrong momma?" the boy asked.

"Never you mind, Micah. Just stay here and if I yell you get to your aunt Mary's right away." When the flaxen-headed boy looked like he would protest a sharp look from his mother stopped him.

She pulled a hatchet from beneath the seat and began to move up the road to round the bend that would bring her in sight of their homestead.

The frame of the cabin was still standing, a blackened skeleton, while the two outbuildings were nothing but piles of sludge.

Her husband was face down ten feet in front of the cabin door, arrows in his back. He had never made it to his gun that she knew he kept on the porch when he worked.

"Little Mary!" the woman screamed. "Jenny! Sally!" She began to move around the edges of the buildings looking for sign on the ground. She cried quietly but the fire that burned in her startling blue eyes screamed her pain.

"Momma?" The tiny voice behind the woman caught her by surprise. She spun to see the twin of her son rising like a soot-covered ghost from the center of the smoldering rubble of the cabin.

"Mary!" The woman ran to the child and snatched her up into a hug that was a hymn of thanks. "Where are the girls?"

"The Chickasaws took them both." The little girl said between sobs. "I was in the bed and papa yelled and Sally made me go down in the root cellar and then I heard more yelling and Sally screamed "Be quiet! And I was. I was so scared Momma until I heard you." The child looked stunned and buried her face into her mother's long black hair. "Where's Papa?"

The woman was already running up the road toward the wagon.

"Hush now, sweetie," she said, "We'll talk about that later."

"Where are we going?" the girl asked.

"First we're going to Auntie Mary's," the woman said, "Then I'm going to get Jenny and Sally back."

CHAPTER ONE

A JOURNEY IN TIME

Mary was feeding the chickens when she heard the sound of the wagon rumbling over the ridge to the east of her cabin. She was a small, slight woman with long blonde hair going to grey. Her eyes were a pale grey and they widened in alarm when she saw her friend Anne's expression and the noted the twins clinging to her with a desperation that was out of character for the self-sufficient children.

Mary could tell, even at the distance, that the darkhaired woman's features were set in a grim expression she had not seen for a long time. Mary set down the feed basket and walked up toward the road, calling back to the house, "There's trouble, Ephraim, better get the guns."

Her husband, who was on the porch carving a hobbyhorse as a gift for a member of their church, did not question her. He rose on his complete left leg, the right missing from the knee down, grabbed his crutch and moved quickly into the cabin.

He re-emerged in a moment with a fowling piece and long rifle tucked under one arm. He stood expectantly scanning the road behind the approaching wagon for signs of danger.

"Indians on the warpath; they have the girls!" Anne called. She reined up the frothing horses and handed the two frightened children down to the blonde woman who hugged each of them fiercely.

Mary looked into the eyes of her friend and volumes passed between them; she knew at once that Anne's husband of two decades was dead; she knew at once that the girls were not, and she knew at once what the two women would do. It was the kind of communication, the knowing of each other's mind and heart that had been instant when they met almost three decades before on the rolling deck of a ship with blood and smoke and the cries of dying men all around them.

The twins flew back to their mother when she had climbed down from the wagon, and she walked toward the cabin holding onto their shoulders with a shuffling step.

"We should send Ephraim into the fort with them," Anne said giving her children a squeeze. "We don't have time to lose."

The quartet stepped onto the shaded porch to join the crippled man.

"It was large party of Chickasaws," Anne said. "They went off North, but they could swing around and attack the river settlements. The villages should be warned."

The two children, despite what they had witnessed, found the hobbyhorse he had been working on fascinating and ventured from their mother's skirts to marvel at it. The adults were grateful for the chance to ignore them for the moment.

Mary put a hand on her husband's arm and looked up into his eyes. "You have to go to Fort Burton and let them know."

"Mary," he said quietly, "You should come in with me."

"No," she said with quiet certainty. "We have to get Jenny and Sally back."

The two longtime spouses looked into each other's eyes; his green and clear, hers grey and smoky. There had always been an unspoken understanding between the spouses that Mary had a tumultuous life before she met him—one that had involved Anne and that had caused her to be put up for transport. She had told him honestly of the child that died still in swaddling in that life but there had been no need to speak of more. For them life was in the now and in their future. And in their daughter.

"You can't go after the girls by yourself," he said quietly, "We have to get the militia."

"No," she said with more force than she meant to. "They'll be too late. Anne and I will get them back."

The two stared at each other for a long moment.

She knew he had lost part of his right leg to a mother bear when he stumbled on her cubs at age nine, but it had never slowed him down; no man for three valleys around dared call him less than whole. He could out hunt, fish or fight most of them, yet she could see in his eyes that question he could not bring himself to ask: *Do you doubt my manhood, my strength to save our child?*

It appeared as if he *would* say it but then he said, "Mary, we have always been honest with everything that mattered; we need to be now. Why not send the militia?"

"It will take too long for them to organize," she said as gently as the urgency of the situation would allow, "and they will lose heart when it will matter most; when things seem impossible or hopeless. They will only pursue Jenny and Sally until it seems too dangerous, or they are too hurt. We will never stop. Never."

He reached out to gently touch her jaw, drawing a finger along it as if memorizing the line of it for some future sculpture. "My little mother bear," he whispered with a gentile smile. "I still feel I should come with you two."

"If we don't come back you will have to come after us," she said. "We'll mark the trail when we can."

She had thought so long ago in Flanders that she had found and lost the only love of her life in Johann, but after she was transported to the new world, she had come to know how lucky she was to find a man like Ephraim. She often felt that the years they had had so far, and their daughter Jenny, were more than she deserved.

"If we fail the girls will need your fire." Mary continued. "And I will need you to avenge me." She captured his hand and kissed it, marveling in the strength in it, rough and raw yet strong and delicate; the hands of an artisan and farmer both. And a lover.

Anne had gone to the wagon and checked the harness on the horses. She removed some of the supplies and farm gear from the back to lighten it. When she had taken out most of the cargo she came up to the porch and walked to her twins who were watching her with apprehension.

"Mary; Micah," she said in a quiet firm voice. "You have to be good for Uncle Ephraim until I come back."

The two children raced to her side and grabbed her skirts. "Don't go, Mama!" they said in unison.

"I need get your sister and Jenny back," she explained. "You have to be strong for momma and take care of your big brother Jason." She leaned down and kissed each on the forehead.

The husband and wife could see the tightness around her mouth as the mother fought to keep from upsetting the twins with her own emotions.

"I better get going," Ephraim took one more, long look at Mary then turned and set the fowling gun and a bag of shot down on the work-table next to his wood carving tools. "This will be better in the woods."

He moved quickly to the wagon and nimbly climbed up to the seat. "Come on, youngins," he called in as cheery a voice as he could manage. "We have to let your Momma and Aunt Mary get going so they can bring Jenny and Sally back." Then he looked at his wife and added, "Come back to me with her if you can but come back."

The children clambered up to the seat on either side of him and clutched on to him as tightly as they had their mother, all three of them fighting tears with equal intensity.

The two women watched the wagon for only a moment and then turned with purpose and went into the barn without a word. They went straight to the back of the barn, past the two empty stalls to where they both knew the thing they sought was kept.

It was a cedar chest, bound with iron and locked with a heavy brass lock.

"Where's the key?" Anne asked.

"I lost it long ago," Mary said. She swung a heavy log splitting maul down hard on the lock. After two swings it snapped off at the hasp. "I prayed I would never have to open this again."

"Save your prayers for those red devils that have our girls," Anne said as she pulled the trunk open. She reached in to draw out a cutlass, her eyes bright as if she were seeing an old lover after a long absence. "They will need them."

CHAPTER TWO

ON THE HUNT

A half hour after they opened the cedar chest the two women were back at Anne's destroyed cabin dressed in clothing from the chest. Both wore short wide trousers, Anne's of leather, Mary's of heavy canvas. Both wore loose cotton shirts girdled with wide belts and both wore soft leather boots that were strapped at the knees.

Anne had a boarding hatchet sheathed in her belt and a brace of pistols worn in holsters slung on a baldric from which hung a wide cutlass.

Mary had a long knife in her belt, a cutlass sheathed on her back and the short fowling gun with powder and shot for it slung in a side pack.

"The devils didn't try to hide their trail," Anne said. It was clear her mind was awhirl. Her eyes raked the woods as if she imagined she saw a naked savage in every shadow.

"They may not care if the militia follows them," Mary said in a church tone. "Or it could be a trap."

Anne knelt by the body of her husband and took a bandana from around his neck. She used the red cloth to pull her black and grey locks away from her face. She kept her eyes on the woods so she would not be captured by the image of her husband Jed lying dead, a good kind man, who had taken her to his heart and into his home knowing her past. He had and her oldest Jason as his own. *I will have tears for you later, Jed*, she thought, *When the girls are safe. Then I will mourn you as you deserve.*

"It will be dark in two hours," Mary said. "But it's a full moon tonight; we should be able to track them by that, if slowly."

"Then let's go." Anne stood next to her friend and the two put hands on each other's shoulders. Anne knew that Mary felt the same guilt as she—the only feeling they both had through the dull numbness of fear for their daughters. It was guilt at the tingle of excitement they both felt for the donning of their old lives. The cutlass had felt so right in her hand, the pistols' weight around her neck as comforting as a babe at her breast.

The two women set off at an easy jog across the clearing and into the

"My little mother bear."

woods following the clear trail the raiders had left. The Indians had used an old deer path with no apparent thought to being followed.

The signs were clear that the girls were with the killers, their shod feet leaving clear marks in the soft earth and several times in the first hour the women saw spots where the children had been allowed to rest, the clear shape of their dresses in crushed grass visible.

"Look here," Mary called to her friend.

Anne did and saw a small wooden cross that had been made by winding grass round two crossed sticks. It had been set in a clump of foliage. It had been hidden hastily but carefully.

"That's from Sally," the blonde-haired mother said.

"She's her father's daughter," Anne said. "She hasn't given up hope; that is for us." The dark haired teen was a religious girl, taking after her father in that. It would be the symbol she would leave and one she believed in strongly.

Her mother had more faith in her own sword arm.

"It's almost dark," Anne said as she picked up the cross and clutched it to her chest as a talisman. "Let's move while we can."

The two raced off deeper into the woods, each scanning a side of the trail by unspoken agreement. Anne discovered a second cross made by her daughter just as the darkness made moving on impossible.

The women dropped to the side of the trail in the last rest space where the girls had been and took sips of water, their first since beginning the run, from a skin that Mary held.

"The moon will be up in a couple of hours," the blonde said.

"They seem to be heading west for their river settlements," Mary surmised. "This track will probably take them most of the way; I think we can chance following it until the moon comes up."

"Ten minutes then?" Mary tossed a handful of jerky to her friend and the other mother nodded. "I'll watch for a couple of minutes."

It was how they used to keep watch on deck, lifetimes ago on the open sea. One would watch while the other napped; they both had the ability to fall instantly sleep and snap instantly wake when they had to.

Anne dozed but in the moment before sleep came, she dreamed, a dream that was a memory.

She saw Calico Jack again for the first time, the handsome rogue who captured her heart and smuggled her onboard his sloop to become a buccaneer. Then in her own right and under her own name as a scourge of the Caribbean. The dreamtime scene skipped ahead to the day the Crown had boarded the ship while the crew, Calico Jack included, were drunk below decks.

It was Anne and Mary back-to-back with swords in hand that opposed the attack and fought until, ringed by steel they were forced to surrender. The long months in the prison cell back in England were all a grey blur except for the grunting of a guard whose face she still refused to recall that she allowed to mount her so she could plead her belly.

She recalled Mary's fever that almost took her before she too could plead a child inside her to keep from the gallows—a child she lost shortly after birth. Jason, now a man was Anne's only good to come from that time.

As her eyes fluttered open she almost imagined she saw Jack one more time as they led him to the gibbet and leaned through the bars to call to him. "If you had fought like man you wouldn't die like a dog!"

Then she realized it was not a dream that there was a figure in the darkness behind Mary.

"Duck!" Anne hissed as she hurled her hatchet with all her might. It whizzed past Mary's head by inches and slammed into the shape beyond her with a meaty impact sound.

Suddenly other dark forms swarmed from the woods and the two women found themselves besieged.

Mary drew her knife and slashed the first figure that reached for her across the throat so swiftly that he could not avoid the cut. He dropped in the way of a second Indian who stumbled.

This allowed the small woman to draw her cutlass and she hacked into the charging brave then stabbed him through the throat with a liquid gurgle.

A brave slammed into Anne's back and bore her to the ground with his body weight. The attacker straddled her and grabbed a handful of her hair. He pressed the back of her head down to smother her face in the soft loom of the forest floor.

Anne heaved up with her powerful arms made strong with lee lines and halyards and kept strong with farm work and unsettled the warrior on her back.

He tumbled to the side, and she rolled over so that for a moment they were face to face on their sides. His eyes were points of light in the dark of the forest, wide with the shock of being upset so easily by a woman.

He launched himself on her again, this time pining her shoulders with both his hands. He leered down at her with a savage grin that turned to shock when she jammed the muzzles of both pistols against his belly and fired them. There were simultaneous muffled explosions, and the brave was propelled off her to collide with another brave.

She was on her feet before the gore soaked second brave recovered from the collision and felled him with a single cutlass blow that split him from crown to jaw.

The two women leapt to stand back-to-back in the sudden silence that followed the bloody violence. The weak starlight was enough to see the shapes piled round them but little else.

They stood hyper alert for several minutes with the only sound their own breathing and the low whimper of the first Chickasaw as his life drained out through his slit throat.

The woods were silent as death for minutes that seemed eternal, but the natural sounds of the night gradually returned, and it became clear to the two women that they had killed all the attackers.

"They left them as rearguards," Anne said in a tight whisper.

"It's why they made the trail so easy to follow." Mary said. "It will be harder now."

"Maybe not. They would be sure these four would either stop a small party or warn them of a larger one."

"Well, they didn't do either," Mary grinned. "So, let's go get our girls."

The women dragged the bodies into the brush on either side of the path, took the powder and shot from them and then headed off down the trail as quickly as they could.

CHAPTER THREE

AMBUSH

The two mothers followed the trail as fast as the darkness allowed until the moon fell. Then they proceeded at a slow walk until shortly before dawn when they were able to move at nearly a full run.

"The girls are slowing them down," Mary noted as she knelt to read the sign "We might overtake them if they have very far to go."

They moved easily, their frontier-hardened bodies ignoring the aches and strains that age and the demands of the journey put on them. With the sun's rising they increased their pace yet again as they could see that the sign that the group they were pursuing had also increased its. Signs showed that the two girls were being dragged more and there were less signs that they had been allowed to rest.

"The red devils are getting closer to home," Anne guessed. "That's why they are quickening their steps."

The two women felt they were close to their children and pushed on through their exhaustion until, at midday they topped a rise and saw a broad flat river plain ahead of them. The Chickasaws had erected a village on the banks of the river with cultivated fields spreading on the East side of the watercourse.

"The girls are there," Anne said aloud what both mothers knew in their heart.

"We can't get much closer during the day," Mary said. "We will have to wait for nightfall." As she said it, even knowing it was the wise course of action she knew it would be the most agonizing hours she would ever spend.

The two hid beneath a tangle of foliage on a ridge that gave them a view of the trail before and behind them and rested through the heat of the afternoon.

The hours crawled by with the adrenaline of the chase giving way to the reality of their age. Anne had birthed five children, Mary two and they were no longer the swashbuckling youths who had ranged the Main under threat of shot and shell.

They both dozed, unable to keep awake despite being closer to the Indian settlement. The afternoon air was crisp and windy but there were still enough leaves on the bushes to screen the two mothers for any casual eyes, so they slept deeply.

Mary woke first, her eyes opening with an immediate understanding of where she was and why. She lay looking up at the screen of foliage and the orange of the late afternoon sky for a long moment. She could hear Anne breathing easily beside her, a comforting sound that brought back nights below decks two decades before.

She thought of the first time she had seen her friend as a darkhaired sea vixen that swept across the decks of the merchant ship where Mary had been disguised as a cabin boy.

It was like a dream more than a nightmare as the cutlass wielding sea tigress dodged through the smoke and shot, hacking down men like wheat. Somehow Mary had not felt fear of the gore-soaked Amazon, but admiration.

Mary had been at war in Flanders both disguised as man a foot and as cavalry but the confined combat of the sea battle, the chaos and confusion, the sense was not that she was afraid, but that she had come home.

It was a sense she had tried to put back in her mind, to hide away with other memories, like the death of her husband in Flanders and losing the child that had allowed her to escape the gallows shortly after his birth.

She shifted on the ground and reached up to brush her blonde hair from her forehead. She looked at her hand, an old woman's hand, yet delicate with long fingers. The knuckles were swollen and red with the farm work that was her life now, but she thought them honest hands.

They had taken life on the red roiling decks and in the muddy fields of the Continent, but they had given it as well, holding her and Anne's squealing children and coaxing green life from the stubborn Carolina soil.

Now, after so long they had taken life again, but in an attempt to save life; the course of her existence was truly a mad one, a book written by an insane deity.

"God," she prayed, "let me save the children; I've had a better life than I could ever have hoped for, lived it on my own terms, even being lucky enough to find Ephraim when I had no right to companionship. Jenny is innocent of my life. Sally has nothing of her mother in her save her will. If you must take a life in all this, take mine."

"We're in this together, Mary," Anne's strong whisper startled the petite woman. She had not realized she was speaking her invocation out loud. She turned to look at her friend.

"So, if there's tariff to be paid, we'll both pay it," the darkhaired woman said, "But I'd rather make those naked devils dance to the piper's tune then any of us." In the gathering twilight Anne's smile was bright and fierce.

"Like it's always been, eh, Annie?"

"Aye, shipmate!" It was the same glint in Anne's eyes and grin on her lips that Mary had seen that first day in the midst of battle, a Valkyrie of the sea ready to send the souls of her foes to the halls of the dead or take the trip herself with equal indifference. And Mary felt the same rush of her blood to her limbs, her sword hand tingling with anticipation.

It was different only because there were lives that mattered in the equation. She knew the thing that had not been spoken between them was an unalterable truth: their daughters must come out of that village, or the two mothers were ready to take them with them on the final journey themselves.

The two sisters of the sword rose together, brushed off their clothes and headed down the trail and into the village to get their children back.

CHAPTER FOUR

PAYING THE RED DEBT

The two mothers stole two blankets from an outlying hut that seemed to be a rest shack for field workers and slipped into the outer ring of the village. The darkness wrapped them both as well as the blankets and their postures were confident so that no one questioned them as they moved deeper into the heart of the enemy settlement.

Mary was careful to keep her blonde hair hidden but Anne's long black hair, now unbound from her husband's scarf, gave no cause of curiosity and was an effective disguise.

They had only the vaguest of plans, to look for gatherings where there might be some celebration of the cabin raid or goal where prisoners might be kept.

The thing that impressed itself on Anne was the sense that they might have been walking through any frontier settlement of their experience: dogs barked and raced about, the men walked to and fro laughing and joking, children squealed and chased each other and played recognizable games like stick and hoop and catch. The Chickasaw women sat before the long houses and gossiped with each other or scolded the children in scenes that might have been women they knew in their own village.

In an irony not lost on the once-buccaneer as she realized the savages she had come to fight as an enemy were human mirrors of her own world.

The realization did nothing to blunt her purpose or give her pause; she would do what she needed to, and she knew Mary would as well.

The rhythm of the village changed as twilight deepened and many moved into their long houses to eat a meal and sit in fellowship. The two mothers kept walking as if with specific destination so as not to draw attention to themselves, but their eyes missed nothing.

Anne noticed a building apart from the others near the riverbank that had a single bored brave standing before it.

"There," Anne indicated the lone figure, "see what I do?"

Mary gave a cold laugh, "A turnkey is always the same world round, eh?"

The two women did their best to not hurry their pace and walked a long loop around the building to find a small stand of trees to conceal themselves until full dark crawled over the settlement.

They watched the Indian until all was black and almost moved in toward the brave when a woman from the village walked out to him with a basket and stopped to give him small bowl and gourd of liquid. They flirted for a few moments then the woman went into the hut.

In the brief moment the curtain door was pulled aside Anne glimpsed figures within, but she could not tell if were the girls. She fought her urge to race across the open space. Mary, who must have sensed her friend's urge, put a restraining hand on her arm.

There was a scream a yell, and the woman came hurtling out the door cursing in her native tongue and holding her arm. The brave laughed pointing at a wound that looked like a bit and the indignant squaw stomped off into the night.

"That's our girls," Anne said with pride.

Despite their situation both women chuckled.

The guard was squatting on the ground in front of the hut to eat his meal, laughing to himself when the mothers walked up to him. He looked up to see what the 'squaws' wanted and Anne split his skull with her hatchet.

"Momma!" Jenny cried as the blonde haired piratess raced into the hut. Anne dragged the guard in and dumped his body before she turned to see her own child.

Their daughters were images of their mothers with Jenny petite and frost haired and Sally buxom and dark. The girls were as fast friends as their mothers had been.

The girls were bound hand and foot with rawhide that ran to a stake in the ground.

Mary sliced them free, and each girl flung themselves into their mother's arms.

"Papa's dead!" Sally wept. "And I don't know about little Mary..."

"She's alright thanks to you," Anne said. She worked hard to harden herself and not cry.

"But Papa!" the girl began.

"Shh, hush now," Anne said. "We have to get out of here; I need you to be strong!" She looked into her daughter's eyes and the girl took a deep breath. Her lip quivered but she nodded her head.

Mary and Jenny were at the door already, arms around each other. The two mothers made eye contact and once again reconfirmed their silent agreement.

"I'll take the lead," Anne whispered. "You girls stay together; we're going to try to get a canoe and head down stream."

The girls held hands, reluctantly releasing their mother's. Then for the first time they noticed how the women were dressed.

"Momma," Sally asked, "Why are you dressed like that?"

"Shh!" Anne said, "Talk later. Be quiet and stay low."

Mary pulled aside the flap door and stepped out.

The moon had risen, and the landscape was in stark relief including the figure of the Indian maiden that Sally had bitten.

The Indian was coming back to the hut with another woman both of whom had long switches in their hands, intent on revenge.

When the Indians saw the figures coming out of the hut, they began screaming immediately to rouse the camp!

Anne reached for her axe to throw but the two Indians turned and ran back toward the main settlement before she could draw and throw.

"Make for the river!" Anne yelled. The four women turned and raced for the bank of the watercourse.

Luck had turned against them, however, for a party of braves was coming back late from a trip up stream and ran for the screaming maidens. This put them between the fugitives and the watercourse.

"This way!" Mary called and the four swerved to head parallel to the river.

There were bodies pouring from the long houses and the din of alarm was spreading.

"We have to get the girls away," Anne said but she could see no way to do it with the roused village in pursuit.

"We'll have to hide the girls," Mary said, "and draw the Indians off."

The four fugitives turned and tried to make it to stand of trees toward the north of the village, but more Chickasaws cut them off. Mary fired her fowling piece which felled three braves and slowed the racing warriors. But there were too many for it to effectively 'blow' an opening for the fugitives to run through.

Instead, the four were forced to an open field that was strewn with boulders that were too big to have been cleared for farming and had been turned into a corral for the few horses that the tribe owned.

Anne looked ahead and saw that the way was blocked by more braves and made decision. "We stand here!" She called when they had come to a sheered-off outcrop of rocks that thrust up from the ground. Two of the basalt boulders joined to an almost right-angled wall.

She spun to put her back to the stonewall and faced the pursuing Indians. "Girls, against the rock." she ordered.

"Momma…" the darkhaired teen began.

"Do it, Sally; they will pay dearly if they want us." She planted her feet as the two teenagers moved into the niche of the rocks.

"Aye," Mary said in a crisp whisper, "In full weight of blood-geld."

The two women stood shoulder-to-shoulder drawing their weapons as the first wave of the braves came upon them.

The howling natives, some barely dressed and lightly armed with war clubs and tomahawks, raced full bore at the two buccaneers expecting to bowl them over by sheer force of presence.

The two mothers gave no ground, however, meeting the charge with determined anger. Their cutlasses moved as if they were a single blade, scything red flesh in geysers.

The charge broke and the warriors that did not fall in the first red rush fell back into a rough semi-circle around the four fugitives.

"Decks clear Starboard," Mary whispered. Her eyes were focused hard on the angry faces that surrounded them.

"Decks clear Larboard," Anne didn't have to look down to see the six dead Chickasaw warriors at their feet. She did not have to look to her right to see Mary's posture; the blonde would be slightly crouched with her knees bent but up on the balls of her feet. Her cutlass would be resting blade up on her right shoulder, long knife held out in front of her chest. There would be a grin on her face as if she were ready to open a present at Christmas.

She didn't have to look because she knew it as if it had happened a thousand times before.

Both women were breathing easy, their pulses racing, but not from fear—Anne sometimes wondered if she could feel fear like others could—but from excitement. It was a feeling that Anne had tried to forget: a moment of life lived so close to the edge of death that all other moments, save perhaps for the moment of her children's birth, paled by comparison. The rest of her life seen from the plateau of that experience was a ghost life.

"They'll try us once more in rush before they fall back and realize they could take us by sheer weight of numbers or arrows, Mary."

"Then we'll teach them the hornpipe, eh, my Bonnie girl?"

Anne laughed, a sound that in the moment caused the sea of red faces watching them to flash with puzzlement.

Then Mary added, "When that last charge comes, I'll take it so you can use the pistols."

Anne knew she meant for the two pistols would be for the girls so that the mothers would know their daughters were safe before the Indians took them down.

Then the darkhaired Amazon realized she could feel fear, but not for herself. And that fear turned to anger as a new war cry went up from the Chickasaw warriors who surged forward.

Mary's gun roared and Anne roared in return. She hacked down with the hatchet as she sliced up with the cutlass, each weapon cleaving an opponent almost in half in a spray of gore that blinded her.

She fought through the blindness and by instinct caught a war club blow on her left shoulder but ignored the pain and ran the attacker who landed it through with her sword.

The second onslaught of braves lasted longer than the first with a more determined press, but the women had chosen their position well. The Indians could not rush them with more than four wide and the press of warriors from the back anxious to get into the battle would not allow those in the front to maneuver.

This was an advantage to the two women who had fought that way on rolling decks so long ago. Their blades whirled as if by one mind in intersecting arcs so that no moccasined foot made it past them.

The buccaneers had guessed wrong about the determination of the Indians and their own ability. The women sustained not only a second charge, but a third onslaught of screaming warriors who came on as fast and hard as they could but were stopped at the same line each time.

The charge broke again, and the braves fell back leaving a pile of dead almost waist high in front of the two warrior mothers.

The front line of the Indians who stood four yards away from the two warriors stared with confused expressions. It was clear that none of them could imagine white men, let alone white women being so fierce.

Anne glanced at her own left shoulder to see where the war club had struck her but could not see the wound for the splatter of gore and guts that covered her. She could feel blood dripping through her hair, but she had no idea if it were her own or her enemies.

She chanced a look over at Mary and for a moment her breath caught. The petite blonde was a scarecrow of gore, her golden hair now dark red and matted, a long gash on her left cheek and her clothes rent and stained. She still had her fighting grin fixed on her face and her eyes shone with a light Anne was sure her own had.

The Indian warriors in front of them were now joined by others who all raised bows to draw on the women but held their fire.

"This will be it," Mary said when she caught the motion of Anne's head to look at her.

"Fair wind," Anne said.

"Fair wind."

It looked as if the bows would be released in the next breath and Anne prepared to turn and empty her pistols at their daughters when a voice from behind called out clear command. The warriors parted for a strange figure to step through.

EPILOGUE

THE RED SISTERHOOD

The tottering figure that moved through the parted line of the braves was a silver haired old woman.

She was wrapped in a blanket that was decorated with shells and trade beads and it was clear from the deference the warriors gave her she was a person of importance.

She moved across the space between the Chickasaw and the escapees in complete silence.

Mary looked over at Anne and realized that dark-haired warrior was badly injured. There were dozens of gashes on her exposed arms and legs, and she was covered in gore.

Anne looked back at her, and she knew she was thinking the same thing; *They can't fire arrows while she is with us: a hostage if we need it.*

It startled the blonde warrior when the old woman spoke in halting English. "You are warriors of great medicine," she said.

"We are mothers and reivers of the sea," Mary said. "Send your braves to feed our swords if you want more of your own mothers to weep, our blades are hungry for more red food."

The old woman looked from woman to woman and then to the two cowering girls beyond. Then the old woman turned to face her people, raised her arms. She spoke several phrases and the bows were lowered.

"Our power is in our children," the old woman said. "This day you have taken much of the power of the Chickasaw people."

"We will take more if you wish to take our children again." Anne said. She looked like one dead already with her clotted hair and red stained face. Her blue eyes were luminous and her voice calm with the promise of more carnage.

The old woman returned her smile with a gentle expression. She pulled a knife from sheath at her waist and made a slice across her skinny left forearm which she held out.

"You have taken the blood of my children, and I give you mine to mingle with yours. Your power will be ours and our strength yours and thus we will know peace for all our days and the days of our children to come."

The two shipmates looked at each other before they slashed themselves across their own forearms to step forward to touch forearms with the little woman.

"Welcome to the red sisterhood," Mary said to the old Indian, "I think we've all paid our dues."

THE END

AN AFTERWORD:
MAKING FRONTIER MAGICK

I've been camping in the deep woods, gone black powder shooting and hiked along the Appalachian Trail in both good and bad weather. I am also lucky enough to live in a state that was at the 'spear tip' of colonization/ frontier life of Europeans in the northeast on this continent so I've seen many of the very places mentioned in some of the Leatherstocking Tales books I grew up reading.

The adventures of Declinn Blayde are a trip through time and into my own heart—a case of many influences coming together to be better than the sum of the parts—I hope.

I grew up on reruns of the Walt Disney *Davey Crockett—King of the Wild Frontier* mini-series and first runs of *Daniel Boone* (come on—you know you started singing the song the second you read this) on television, the *Northwest Passage* tv series and several versions of Fennimore Cooper's Leather Stocking Saga.

And in books, *Drums Along the Mohawk, Northwest Passage, Last of the Mohicans* and Conan.

Conan, you say? How'd that mighty thewed Cimmerian slip in there?

Well, Robert E. Howard, Conan's pappy loved the rugged pioneers that 'tamed' the west and those same Leather Stocking Tales I enjoyed. When he set about writing his tales of the Aquilonian frontier he tapped into those pioneer adventures and married with the sword and sorcery of the rest of his world.

It was that grounded, realistic wilderness adventure infused with the magicks of Hyboria that inspired me to create Declinn Blayde and his world of both the real and the fantastic.

I consider the American Frontier up to about the Alamo in the 1830s- when reliable pistols came in—to be the swashbuckling period of our history. It is therefore only natural that I decided to do some swashbuckling tales sent in the woods.

Tomahawk and Sorcery is what I call it and if you like it there will be more tales that explore a mythology you may not have thought about before and the life of frontier artist adventurer Declinn Blayde.

And the tale of Anne and Mary written here is my 'what if' tale that combines my love of the pirate films and books like *Captain Blood*, the dynamic heroines created by Robert E. Howard—his version of Red Sonya—

from “Shadows of the Vulture”, “Belet of Queen of the Black Coast” from the Conan tale and Dark Agnes.

I hope you enjoy the swashbuckling and come back for more…

Teel
03/03/2025

ABOUT OUR CREATORS

WRITER -

TEEL JAMES GLENN has killed hundreds and been killed more times—on stage and screen, as he has traveled the world for forty-plus years as a stuntman, swordmaster, storyteller, bodyguard, actor, and haunted house barker.

He has dozens of published novels, and his poetry and stories have been printed in over two hundred magazines, including *Weird Tales, Mystery, Pulp Adventures, Mad, Black Cat Weekly, Cirsova, Silverblade, Heroic Fantasy, Blazing Adventures,* and *Sherlock Holmes Mystery.*

His novel *Not Born of Woman* was a Shamus, Silver Flachion and Pulp Factory finalist for best novel in 2023. His novel *A Cowboy in Carpathia: A Bob Howard Adventure* won Best Novel 2021 in the Pulp Factory Award. He is also the winner of the 2012 Pulp Ark Award for Best Author. He was a finalist for the Derringer Short Mystery Award in 2022. His novel, *Callback for a Corpse,* was a second-place winner in the CWR Poll as best mystery.

His website is: TheUrbanSwashbuckler.com

INTERIOR ILLUSTRATIONS -

MIKE LAPERUTA - is a New York–based illustrator and cartoonist whose work spans comics, painting, sculpture, caricature, and design. He holds degrees in Computer-Aided Graphic Design and Art Education and brings a strong foundation in both traditional and digital media to his storytelling-driven artwork. Mike has collaborated with companies including Topps, Upper Deck, Dynamite Entertainment, Fleer, Typhoon Productions, Breygent, Cryptozoic, RRPARKS and 5FINITY, with additional contract work connected to Marvel, DC Comics, Nickelodeon, Hasbro, Disney, and Kevin Smith. His creative career also includes teaching illustration, commercial design, and public art projects. Passionate about character and narrative, he continues to develop original comics and sketchcards. You can find more of Mike's work on Ebay and his Whatnot shows. his Instagram: @mikelaperuta

COVER ARTIST -

ADAM BENET SHAW–Accomplished painter, illustrator, and comics creator, Adam has garnered acclaim across a number of artistic media. After completing studies at the Cleveland Institute of Art in Ohio, the Edinburgh College of Art in Scotland and Watts Atelier in California, Shaw was selected as an emerging American artist to watch by European gallery owners and exhibited in London, England. He has been featured in "New American Painting", selected multiple times for the Arkansas Art Center's Delta Exhibit, and shown at the prestigious "Red Clay Survey" at the Huntsville Museum of Art. His work has also been shown in over 50 group and solo shows in the US and internationally. His figurative paintings are a prominent part of a 140-foot mural entitled "The History of Cotton" at the National Cotton Exchange Museum, St. Jude's Children's Research Hospital, the National Contact Bridge Museum, and a treasured part of private and corporate collections. He has created storyboards for several motion pictures, including Paramount Pictures' film "Black Snake Moan" directed by Craig Brewer, stage design for operas and corporate events, and character illustrations for the gaming industry. His published graphic novel work includes the series "Dead In Memphis", "Bloodstream" for Image Comics, "David: The Illustrated Novel" from Shepherd King Publishing and "Harpe: America's First Serial Killers" from Cave-in-Rock Publishing. He shares his love of art through teaching and workshops at his studio in the Broad Avenue Arts District in Memphis. Recently he has been painting book covers for pulp publishers Pro Se Productions and Airship 27 Productions.

www.ingramcontent.com/pod-product-compliance
Lightning Source LLC
LaVergne TN
LVHW010922110826
845149LV00013B/2451